ART OF Affection

ELLEN BUTLER

Author of *Heart of Design* and *Planning for Love*

Published by
Crimson Romance
an imprint of F+W Media, Inc.
10151 Carver Road, Suite 200
Blue Ash, OH 45242. U.S.A.
www.crimsonromance.com

ISBN 10: 1-4405-8369-2
ISBN 13: 978-1-4405-8369-8
eISBN 10: 1-4405-8370-6
eISBN 13: 978-1-4405-8370-4

This is a work of fiction. Names, characters, corporations, institutions, organizations, events, or locales in this novel are either the product of the author's imagination or, if real, used fictitiously. The resemblance of any character to actual persons (living or dead) is entirely coincidental.

Cover art © iStockphoto.com/AK2, Farbzauber.

*To those who put their lives on the line
every day to serve and protect.*

Acknowledgments

First and foremost, I want to give a hearty thank you to John DeMaria, a detective with more than thirty-four years of experience on the police force. I would have been lost without his expertise and advice. Any sort of embellishments of legal procedures in the book are my own fictional license. Additionally, thanks to Julie Sturgeon, my editor, who has been a trooper working with me to get the kinks out of the *Love, California Style* storylines and into publication on time. As always, thanks to my family for their continued support of my writing.

Chapter One

My Kia rolled to a stop in front of the valet stand at the Spanish-style estate.

"Okay, I just pulled into the drive. I'll see you in a minute." I removed the Bluetooth headset from my ear and tossed the keys to a red-jacketed attendant as I stepped from the car, slinging both handbag and camera over my shoulder.

I'd forgotten the address for Poppy's engagement party and called my sister, Sophie, to direct me the last ten minutes of the, thankfully, uneventful drive. The front windows glowed with lights, creating an inviting feel to the stone and red-tiled mansion, and I snapped a picture to capture the mood. My heels clacked along the stone floors as a doorman pulled the heavy oak door aside for me. A large, sweeping staircase met my sight, and sounds of the party drifted down from the back of the house. I came to an abrupt halt as a tall, black man in a white tuxedo greeted me at the foot of the stairs.

"Your invitation, ma'am."

"Sure, it's right here in my ..." *Oh dear.* I'd forgotten to transfer the white vellum invitation into my evening bag. I could picture it, in my mind, sitting on the foyer table. "Nuts. I guess I left it at home." I shrugged and gave him a winning smile.

"You can't enter without an invitation," he said politely but firmly.

"Oh come on, don't you have a list or something? I've got ID."

He smiled tolerantly but shook his head.

"Look, the host, Poppy, is my sister's best friend. She asked me to take photos for her." I held up my camera. Back in college, I'd lamented my inability to bring the pictures in my head to life on canvas in the way I longed to do, which was what led me to becoming a connoisseur of art rather than a true artist and the reason I worked as a curator at Le Pinceau. However, after my daughter was born, I found creative solace in my photography.

In a blink, the camera was snatched out of my hand, and my anger flashed white hot. "Hey, pal. Be careful with that. What do you think you're doing?"

"There is no photography allowed, and you many not enter without an invitation." He held it above his head as I tried to grab it back.

Refusing to be a part of an undignified keep-away game, I stepped back.

"Fine." I held out my hand. "I'll leave, but not without my camera."

The gatekeeper took his sweet time examining the camera, and then eyed my tapping foot before returning the camera to my outstretched palm. I paced back to the giant front door and called Sophie.

"Where are you? I thought you said you were pulling up. Poppy is asking about you." Party sounds filtered through her phone.

"I forgot the stupid invitation, and the dragon at the gate won't let me through," I said through clenched teeth.

"What?"

"I said," raising my voice to full volume, "the gatekeeper won't let me through!" I glared at said gatekeeper, but my glare didn't seem to move him.

"Cripes, I'll send someone to come get you."

"Thanks." I hung up, crossed my arms, and put on a patient face. A minute later, Ian, my sister's gorgeous fiancé, strode down the steps in a beautifully cut black suit and tie. If I had any interest in men, I would have been insanely jealous of Sophie's good luck in hooking a hunk like Ian. He played Ryder McKay on the popular cop show, *LA Heat*. However, I was simply happy someone came to rescue me.

"You're looking lovely, m'dear. Sophie sent me to slay the dragon." His Irish accent rolled across me as he flashed a grin. *Sophie was right; he did have a perfect Hollywood smile.*

"This numbskull won't let me through." I pointed a finger at the offending dragon.

"Leave off, Alphonso, she's with me." He held out an arm. "My lady, dragon slayed. Come and join us."

I hooked a hand through Ian's elbow, but before I could take a step on one stair, a hand halted us by wrapping around my arm.

"What the ..." Ian muttered as I pulled to a standstill.

"*Don't touch me!*" I screeched at Alphonso, slapping at his hand with my purse. No one, I mean, no one manhandled me.

He immediately released my arm as though he'd been burned.

"Don't touch the lady," Ian said in a low, menacing tone. Ian had been at my sister's house the day I arrived from Las Vegas with cuts and bruises, courtesy of my ex-husband, and he was acutely aware of my aversion to being touched, especially by men, without permission.

Alphonso stepped back with his arms up.

"What's the problem, mate?" Ian asked.

"No cameras. You'll have to leave it with security until the end of the night."

"The hell you say," I snapped.

"Ms. Reagan's orders. She didn't want the paparazzi ruining the party. No cameras."

"Bloody hell, everyone's got a camera on their flippin' mobiles, man. You're not taking them away, are you?"

He shrugged.

"Poppy specifically requested I bring this for her party." I enunciated very slowly, as if speaking to a stubborn child.

"There you go, mate. Poppy asked for it." Ian turned to proceed up the stairs, except Alphonso ran ahead of us and held up his hand to halt our progress.

"I'm sorry, you can't go up until I get this cleared."

"Then get on the bloody horn and get it cleared, man. I haven't got all fuckin' night!" Ian lost his patience.

Alphonso cringed and pulled out a phone. "I have a woman by the name of …" He raised his eyebrow at me.

"Holly Hartland!" I yelled into the receiver.

"Um, Ms. Hartland has a camera. She says Ms. Reagan asked her to bring it. Can you confirm this for me? Yes, I'll wait."

"Holly! Ian!" A voice from the balustrade called down to us. "What are you doing? Poppy's waiting for you! Hurry up." We glanced up to find Poppy's right-hand woman and newly named partner of her party planning business leaning over the railing, her blond locks streaming past her shoulder.

"Cody!" I waved. "This nincompoop won't let me through with my camera. Do you know if Poppy still wants me to take photos?"

"Yes, of course. Alphonso!" she barked, "Get the hell out of the way!"

Alphonso moved to the side, and Ian and I scampered up the stairs, through a large reception room, and out onto the back patio filled with tables of guests. Twinkle lights strung through the shrubbery and the railings, along with the outdoor heaters, gave the party a soft glow. The music had stopped, and the sound of the ocean waves played in the background.

My sister, in a lovely green swing dress, descended upon us. "What the hell took so long?"

Ian released me to kiss her cheek. "Don't ask, luv. We're here now. What's the big announcement?"

"I don't know. Poppy just told the band to take five. Come with me; she asked us to come to the stage."

We found Poppy and her adorable fiancé, Dr. Adam Patterson, with his arm around her waist, surrounded by other party guests, chatting amiably. Poppy looked stunning in flowy, long-sleeved, aquamarine dress that set her red hair off beautifully. Adam's sandy hair shone under the lights, and he looked striking in a dark suit and tie.

Cody approached the group and swished her hand as if presenting a gift from the *Price is Right* show. "Voilà. I found her."

Poppy smiled at us, and in a single swoop, I was enveloped by Chanel No. 5. "I'm so glad you were able to make it. You had us worried."

"Sorry, there was a skinned knee, bloodstains, and a change of outfit at the last minute."

"Ah." Her face turned serious. "Is she okay?"

"Yes, it was Annie. She'll be fine." I waved away her concern. "Gary took care of it."

"Is he here?" She looked past me. "I thought he was your plus-one?"

"Our babysitter bailed and my nanny, Sanvi, is out of town this weekend." I shrugged. "He drew the short straw."

"Shame. You two make such a cute couple. I was looking forward to seeing if our oh-so-serious-detective would let down his hair and party with us."

She wiggled her eyebrows at me, and I could feel my face burn as I shook my head. I didn't have that type of relationship with Gary, the single father with whom I shared a nanny and babysitting chores for my daughter, Eva, and his, Annie. Although on more than one occasion, Poppy had made similar sly comments about us being together.

"Oh well, it can't be helped." She clapped her hands. "Okay, all of you stay right here while Adam and I make our announcement."

Adam helped her onto the stage, and a moment later, a tap-tap-tap on the microphone filled the room. "Hello, is this thing working?"

The audience nodded and a few souls shouted out, "Yes!"

"As most of you know, my mom's been going through some hard times."

My stomach dropped. *Oh no.*

"Well, you'll be happy to hear the new medication she's on seems to be working. We're beating back the cancer!"

Whoops and joyful yells went up through the crowd. I snapped a picture of the couple on stage, turned and found Poppy's mom, Amalina, sitting at a nearby table, with a wobbly smile, holding her husband's hand. He looked down at her with such a look of love I snapped a series of photos.

"Thanks to all of you who have been so supportive with your prayers, and meals, and driving her to appointments." Poppy's smile wavered, and Adam wrapped a possessive arm around her waist while she took a moment to compose herself. "We'd also like to welcome Adam's family and thank all of you who came from out of town to be with us. We feel truly blessed that you're here."

Clapping filled the room.

"But I have one more announcement."

"You're pregnant!" A man's voice piped in from the back.

Adam rolled his eyes and leaned into the microphone. "No, Luke. Please disregard my brother's asinine comments, folks."

"You've been brought here under false pretenses," Poppy said.

A murmur went through the crowd and I lowered the camera.

"Hey, I ain't paying for the lobster dinner. I didn't bring my credit card," someone from the crowd cried. Laughter followed the comment.

Poppy and Adam grinned and she shook her head. "No worries, the food is all paid for. No, you were told this was an engagement party. Well … it's not."

A mumbling of "what" went through the crowd.

"It's a wedding!"

The crowd was stunned to silence for about ten seconds, and then cheers and whistles erupted.

"A moment," Poppy shushed the crowd. "Even though my mother is improving, it occurred to Adam and me that nothing in this world is assured, and we didn't want to wait another moment before tying the knot."

People murmured and nodded with understanding.

"And," Poppy continued, "since you're all dressed up so nice and everything, we figured … what the hell? So why don't you get another cocktail and meander back to your seats—the wedding will start in about fifteen or twenty minutes. Thank you."

Clapping commenced, and my camera whirred, snapping photos of the happy couple and the friends that surrounded them.

Sophie flung her arms around Poppy as soon as she stepped off the stage. I caught the surprise and joy in Poppy's face as she accepted the embrace.

"I can't believe it! You'll be married before me!"

Poppy stepped back. "I still want you and Cody to be my attendants. Adam has his brother. Walter was supposed to be here but got called away on an emergency, so Ian's agreed to stand up with him. And Holly," she turned to me, "would you …"

I was way ahead of her. Holding up my camera, I grinned. "Already on it."

"Thank you, so much. I figured if I hired one of my regular photographers, the secret would get out. Besides, you have such an eye for composition."

I warmed at the compliment. I'd never photographed something as important as a wedding, but the camera gave me every confidence I could capture what Poppy needed.

Poppy's mother joined us with a knowing smile and a hug for her daughter. I had a feeling she'd been in on the secret.

"Boys"—Poppy pointed to Adam and Ian—"go get ready. Ladies, follow me." She hooked her arm through her mother's and gleefully led us à la the Pied Piper. I trotted behind, snapping pictures capturing the crowd's excitement, until we reached a small reception room inside the mansion. A wall of mirrors mounted the far side, and on a stand in the center stood a spectacular wedding gown crafted in lace and tulle with a deep V in the front and back. Wide lace straps and a short train completed a stunning designer gown I could have sworn I'd seen on the front cover of a magazine recently while standing in the grocery checkout line.

"Oh, Poppy, it's just beautiful." Sophie gushed. She, Cody, and her mom rotated around the manikin, viewing the dress from all sides.

"Where did you get it on such short notice?" I asked.

Poppy's eyes gleamed as she watched her friends ooh and ahh. "The designer owed me one, and she happened to have this in my size because the client she originally made it for called off the wedding. A few adjustments and there you have it. Dream wedding dress on the fly."

"Who'd you get to perform the ceremony last minute?" I asked as her mother began unbuttoning the tiny seed pearls.

Poppy's face turned pink. "Do you remember hearing about my blind date who wanted to take me skydiving?"

"Right. Sophie told me all about the hottie bad boy, but you chickened out at the last minute."

"Indeed. Campbell, my aborted skydiving date, is an online minister. A few weeks ago, Adam and I decided to make this happen, and we found out the minister we'd originally planned to have marry us was already booked for another wedding, and … well, Campbell's name came to mind. Luckily, he was available."

"So a bad blind date is going to marry you."

"It wasn't a bad date per se."

"Didn't you kiss him?"

"Uh. Sort of." Her face flamed.

I grinned at her discomfort. "Does Adam know?"

She shot daggers my way. "He knows what he needs to know."

I made a zipping motion across my lips and took a photo as her mom and Cody managed to finish undoing the buttons and remove the dress from its perch.

"Darling, you're not undressed yet," Amalina chastised. "Hurry up; you don't want to keep the groom waiting."

While Poppy undressed, I put the camera down and stepped out for a moment to call Gary with the news.

"So, they just turned the engagement party into their wedding?" he asked in a disbelieving voice.

"Yes. Isn't it exciting? Now I'm really sorry you couldn't come tonight."

"Me too. I'm missing steak and lobster tail."

I snorted. "Men. Is that all you can think about? Two people are getting married at the spur of the moment. It's so romantic."

"Romance, shmomance. I'm going to be dreaming about the lobster I'm missing. I had pizza with two toddlers, you know. You'd better bring me back a piece of cake or something."

I laughed. "Will do. And thanks again for taking one for the team tonight."

"Anytime. You know I owe you one." His voice turned serious. "Or half a dozen after all the times I've dropped Annie off at your place."

"Nonsense. You don't owe me anything. That's what friends are for. Right?"

"Friends ..." He mumbled something unintelligible.

"What?"

"Nothing. Listen, don't drink and drive. Call a cab if you need to, and I'll take you to get your car in the morning."

"Yes, Dad, I'll be careful," I said sarcastically.

"I'm not your dad, Holly. I'm a cop, and this isn't a joking matter."

I winced at his sharp tone and immediately turned on my conciliatory voice. "You're right. I'm so sorry; please don't get mad." I hated arguments and avoided them at all costs. Arguments led to anger, and anger led to violence.

A sigh blew across the phone lines. "Holly, I'm not mad. I just take drinking and driving seriously ... I can hear you cringing. Stop it. I'm not Omar," he said quietly, his voice full of compassion.

Why is it my nerves can rise to the surface so quickly? It had been over a year since Omar went to jail, yet every once in a while, the knee-jerk reaction still came out whenever someone spoke sharply to me. The rational part of me knew Gary was simply concerned for my welfare.

Air flowed in my nose and out my mouth before I answered. "I know. Old habits are hard to break. I'm sorry."

"Don't be sorry. Just realize I'm not like him. I never will be. Now, I'll keep the girls with me tonight, and you can pick Eva up in the morning,"

Sophie stuck her head out and winked at me. "Holly, she's ready for her photo shoot."

Inner poise regained, I gave her a thumbs up. "That sounds good, Gary, thanks. I'm needed, so I've got to run. I'll see you in the morning."

"Be careful."

"I will."

• • •

The evening went off without a hitch ... at least as far as the guests could tell. If possible, the dress looked even more stunning on Poppy's tall, willowy body than it did hanging on the manikin. Her red hair hung in waves down her back, and the cream coloring in the dress only enhanced her alabaster skin. Cody had applied touch of peach lipstick to finish the look. My camera shutter fluttered away, capturing the touching nuance of a first-time bride.

Poppy's diminutive mother walked her down the aisle to a beaming Adam, who had changed into a tuxedo. He and the groomsmen wore mini orchid boutonnieres and stood to the right of the most unlikely looking minister I'd ever seen. Campbell, who held a job as a stunt man, was handsome as sin, with coffee-colored hair down to his shoulders and a devil-may-care look about him. Not at all the staid minister you'd expect. He was perfect for Poppy's unorthodox wedding.

As the bride and groom took their vows, my mind traveled back to my wedding to Omar when I was an excited, young newlywed filled with expectations for happily-ever-after. Even though the warning signs that the marriage would turn abusive were there, I blithely ignored them. Unfortunately, not only did I pay the price for my stupidity, so did my sister.

Campbell's voice interrupted my depressing thoughts. "You may kiss the bride."

I whipped the camera up and captured the iconic moment that begins a couple's life together.

• • •

Because I'd been so busy capturing Poppy's impromptu wedding, I hadn't had time to drink much more than half a glass of champagne and was perfectly sober to drive home. I thought no more about my first marriage until sitting silently in the car. Sophie had once told me that I would find love again and marry the right person. I remember her saying it with a wink and a smile, as though she knew something I didn't. However, my fears of trusting another man with my happiness or my daughter's ran bone deep.

Poppy had pointed out that I trusted my daughter with Gary.

She was right. I absolutely trusted Gary with my daughter. He, like I, treated the girls equally with love and tenderness. Our parenting techniques complimented each other, and the girls had come to respond to both of us as authority figures in their lives. But, as for any kind of romantic feelings for Gary ... I banished those thoughts immediately. My need to rely on Gary was too important for me—and the girls—to go down some sort of foolish romantic road.

Although ... there were a few times when he'd given me that intent look—like just before I left him at the house tonight. His expression had turned soft, almost sympathetic, with his brows up and his jaw muscle flexed. A little flutter had tickled my throat; it wasn't quite unease, but something close to it. I'd caught him examining me like this maybe a half dozen times in the past few months. It seemed as though something burned in his brain and he was trying to figure out how to tell me. I couldn't decide if the look was good or bad, but there seemed to be a bit of wariness in his expression, which led to my discomfort. I never dared to say anything, instead waited patiently for him to speak. Invariably, one of the girls would interrupt or Gary would give his head a shake, and the moment would be lost.

I pulled to a halt at the red light and sighed. Poppy was married, Sophie engaged and planning a wedding. The thought of getting remarried was an enigma to me. I hadn't even reached thirty, yet it seemed as though I was destined to remain single. The years of loneliness suddenly stretched ahead like the empty road in front of me.

Chapter Two

"Wait, it's not in the hole—can you straighten it up a bit?" I leaned farther forward from my perch on the step stool.

"Not really. Hang on, let me try something."

"Oh, that's better … just a little more to the left. No, too far. Hold up. There, I think we got it." The dowel made contact with the hole and slid into place with a thunk. "That's it." I leaned back and the Christmas tree started shaking, so I grabbed the top to keep it steady. "Geez. What are you doing?"

Gary's head was buried in the plastic branches halfway down the tree. "I'm looking for the plug. It's supposed to be around here."

Yesterday, Gary and Annie had come over to help decorate my little six -foot, fake tree, which fit perfectly in a corner of the family room. With the patience of a saint, Gary had sat on the floor, detangling and then stringing yards of multicolored lights while the girls decorated the lower half with non-breakable ornaments. The few glass ornaments I owned were hung higher up, where little hands couldn't reach them. The girls finished it off with yards of red ribbon that I'd purchased from a local craft store.

When we finished decorating my tree, Annie begged her daddy to get a tree. Originally, Gary told me he planned to buy a real one, but when I asked if he'd remember to water it daily, he decided the convenience of a fake couldn't be beat. So, after eating dinner with us, Annie and Gary left for the local hardware store armed with the weekend sale flyer and a credit card.

"Mommy, how come our tree isn't so big?" Eva asked.

"Everyone's tree is different, pumpkin," I answered, making an effort to keep the laughter out of my voice.

The new tree was either a testament to Annie's persuasiveness or Gary's inability to gauge the height of his ceiling; the eight-and-a-half-foot, pre-lit fir touted 2,000 LED lights and barely fit into their living room. Gary set it up in a corner near the front window, but the branches still protruded a good portion into the seating area. He plugged the last strand into the central line, pressed the switch, and the room lit up. I blinked at the brightness and swore the rest of the house lights dimmed as the tree sucked up electricity. I think it may have been humming.

"Oh, Daddy. It's perfect! Don't you think, Eva?" Annie clapped her hands in delight.

"Pretty." Eva nodded.

"Wow. That's really bright." I bit my lips.

Gary stood back with his hands on his hips. "It didn't look this big in the store."

"It never does." A snicker slipped out. Gary shot a look at me, and I coughed in my hand to cover up my merriment.

"Daddy, can we put up the star?" Annie held up an unopened box with a light-up gold star.

I kept my hand over my mouth as Gary looked at the topmost branch, which scraped the ceiling.

"I don't think it's going to fit up there. The tree is a bit taller than I thought."

"But, Daddy, I picked it out special."

"I know, but I just don't think it'll work. I'm sorry, sweetie."

Poor Annie's face crumpled and my heart went out to her.

"Here, why don't you give me the star?" I held out my hand. "Your dad and I will see what we can work out while you and Eva start decorating the tree."

Almost a dozen small boxes of ornaments littered the floor. The girls didn't have to be asked twice; they ripped open the one closest to the tree and set to work.

I took the star out of its Fort Knox-style wrapping and twisted it around in my hands. The star had a wire that could be plugged into one of the LED sockets on the tree's light string so it would illuminate in all its yellow glory.

Fifteen minutes later, armed with some wire and a little ingenuity, I climbed the stepladder to attach the star. I wobbled for a moment and Gary leapt forward, wrapping his hands around my waist to steady me. His touch, though completely nonsexual, warmed me and unexpectedly sent prickles along my shoulders. Besides a few light touches in passing, it was the first time he'd put his hands on me since he found me curled up in the corner of my room having a panic attack last winter after I read some hate mail from my in-laws. A mortifying position I'd sworn he'd never see me in again. Even though the odious letters from Omar's family continued to arrive on a monthly basis, I'd never allowed them to overcome me like they did the night Gary found me.

Once I finished wiring up the star, he released me and stepped back to allow me to descend.

"What do you think?" To cover up my discomfort, I glanced between the tree and the children. Anywhere but at Gary.

Annie clapped her hands. "I love it. Now I can show Mommy if she comes home for Christmas."

"I want a star, Mommy," Eva said pushing a dusky blond curl out of her eye.

"Don't you like the pretty white angel Nana gave you for Christmas last year? It's very special."

"Oh, right." Star forgotten, Eva went back to her decorating.

"Daddy, I'm done," Annie announced. "Can I go watch *Winnie the Pooh*?

"Me too," Eva agreed and skipped out of the room.

Gary and I surveyed the unopened ornament boxes.

"Girls, you've hardly started. What about all those boxes?" He pointed to the pile.

"You and Miss Holly can do it." Annie shrugged and followed Eva.

With a look of disbelief, Gary watched his daughter go as I bit back more laughter. His dark eyes swung back to me. "Go ahead. Laugh."

"Who, me?" I asked wide-eyed. "There is nothing funny here."

He crossed his arms and looked at the barely decorated tree. "I honestly don't know what I was thinking. They had this damn thing on display, Annie saw it and fell in love, and I just opened my wallet and said to myself, 'It's Christmas; she should have what she wants.' You know, her mother was always hesitant to decorate because she never knew if she'd have the energy to put it away after the holiday. Her depressions were always worse afterward." He ended in a quiet tone. His marriage ended at the beginning of the year when his manic-depressive wife left Annie with a babysitter and a Dear John letter on the mantel.

"Have you told her Claire isn't coming home?"

"Yes, I had a conversation with her in the car. She says she understands, but I'm sure in her five-year-old mind she just can't grasp that her Mommy won't be home for Christmas." He rubbed his eyes. "Although I know in my head we're better off without her, there are days I want to throttle Claire for what she did to that kid."

I didn't blame him, knowing in my head that Gary would never physically harm her given the chance. "I'm sorry. What can I do?"

"Nothing you're not already doing. Christ, you're a better mother to her than Claire ever was." He stared up at the monstrous shrub. "Now what the hell am I going to do about this tree?"

He looked so adorably confused and dejected that I reached out and patted his shoulder. "Don't worry, we'll get it decorated and the girls will be so thrilled. It'll put my sad little tree to shame."

"Some days," he pinched his nose, "I wonder what the hell I'm doing raising her on my own."

I'd struggled with similar thoughts; however, in my situation, Omar's abusiveness could not be tolerated. "First, you're a great dad. Annie loves you. Second, you're not on your own. You have me, and Eva, and Sanvi."

"You're right, of course. I don't know what I'd do without you."

"Aw, shucks." I bumped shoulders with him. "It's nothing."

"I'm serious, Holly. I don't know where I'd be without you."

The look was back. Those solemn hazel eyes studied me and he was so close I could feel his breath brush my cheek. Both fear and a touch of excitement prickled along my spine.

• • •

Gary could see the flecks of gold surrounding her iris, and her light lemony scent drifted about him. Her soft lips, so close, parted slightly, and he could see a pulse fluttering at her neck. *She looks so kissable; do I dare?* His head warred with his body. He knew she didn't see him in any sort of romantic light. There was no reason she should either. After all, he was just a cop … okay, detective. But, as he'd learned from his first disastrous marriage, cops weren't so great with relationships, and Holly wasn't the type of woman with whom you had a one-time roll in the sack. *But would stealing just one kiss irrevocably shift the relationship?*

"Holly … I …"

"*Eva, no.* That's mine." A slapping sound and a cry rent the air.

Moments later, Eva came running into the room, babbling and sobbing all at once, and flung herself into her mother's arms. Gary turned and strode into the playroom to deal with his daughter while Holly calmed Eva. This wasn't the first, nor would it be the last, time the girls had a contretemps. Their lives were so entwined that they often behaved like sisters, which included the unhappy reality of bickering. In the end, the adults determined both the girls were at fault. He sent Annie to her room, and Eva had to sit on the stairs for a time-out.

When he returned, it was to find Holly busy hanging decorations on the ginormous bush. He watched for a moment as she hummed to herself, and marveled how lucky he was to have such an amazing person in Annie's life. He wasn't kidding when he told her he didn't know what he'd do without her. When Claire first left him, he'd called in the cavalry, and his parents had flown out immediately to help with Annie, but everyone knew the situation to be temporary. Holly stepped into the role not only of concerned friend, but also pseudo-mother to his daughter, who was sad and confused about why Mommy was gone and when she'd come back.

Holly reached up high, and her shirt rode up above her waist, showing a slim line of skin. Gary forced himself to remain still, even though a part of him longed to touch the softness at the small of her back. He'd been foolish to consider risking the comfortable camaraderie they shared. His daughter's happiness was far more important than a momentary lapse of sexual arousal.

With an inward sigh, he opened a new ornament box and set to work. After her time-out, Eva returned to help with the tree, and Annie returned to her movie. When the ornaments were on and gold garland strung, the tree's glow seemed less blinding.

Eva sat on the couch curled up on her mother's lap, both of them watching the tree. "How many more days until Santa comes?"

"Oh, about twenty more days, pumpkin." Holly snuggled her daughter. "Guess who's coming to visit at Christmas?"

"Nana!"

"That's right."

"Annie, come in and see your tree," Gary called.

Annie, her dark curls bouncing, thundered into the front room and skidded to a halt. "Daddy, it's like in *The Nutcracker*. I love it." She flung herself against his leg.

"I'm glad you like it." Gary crouched down and lifted his daughter into his arms.

"What's that?" She pointed.

"That is a frame and it says, 'My fifth Christmas.' We'll take a picture of you on Christmas Day and put it in there."

"Will Aunt Sophie and Uncle Ian be there, too?" Eva asked Holly.

"Yes, of course," she replied.

"What about Annie and her daddy?"

He watched as Holly glanced up at him. "We'll have to ask. They may have plans with their own family."

"Can Annie come over for Christmas?" Eva asked Gary.

"Yeah, Daddy, can we?" Annie looked expectantly at her father.

Gary shifted uncomfortably, unwilling to outright deny the request. "I'm sure we can work something out. Don't forget, Gammy and Pop Pop are coming to visit us." He tweaked her pert little nose.

"What about Auntie Caroline and my cousins?"

"Not this year, sweetie. Just Gammy and Pop Pop." He put her back down. "Who wants a snack after all that hard work?"

"I do." Eva scrambled off her mother's lap and grabbed his hand.

Annie remained staring at the tree. "Not now."

Gary escorted little Eva into the kitchen, set her up with some milk and graham crackers, and left her at the table, her stubby little fingers dunking squares into the milk. He stopped just outside the front room doorway to find his precious daughter on the couch snuggled up with Holly where Eva had been only minutes before.

She brushed curls away from Annie's face. "I don't know if your mommy will come home, sweetie. What did your Daddy say about it?"

"He said she's not going to be here. That she's far away, across the ocean, and we can't see her."

"Well, then I think you should trust what your daddy said."

"Do you think she's still mad at me and that's why she won't come home?"

Gary felt as though he'd received a punch to the gut and couldn't seem to take another step.

"Annie, why would you think that? Your mommy didn't leave because she was mad at you." Holly pulled her closer.

"Yes, she did." Annie sniffled. "Don't tell Daddy, but I broke the lamp in her bedroom and she was mad. Then a few days later she was gone."

Gary sucked wind and seemed frozen in place.

"Oh, baby, no. That's not why your mommy left. Sometimes adults do things for all sorts of reasons that may not make sense to you. But she didn't leave because you broke a lamp."

"Was she mad at Daddy because he's a policeman?"

Holly took a deep breath before answering. "I don't know exactly why your mommy left, but I know it's not because of anything you did. Understand? You're a smart, beautiful little girl. And I feel so lucky that you've become part of our family, with Eva and me."

"And my daddy?"

"Your daddy, too."

"Do you think you and Daddy can get married? Then Eva and I can be real sisters and live in your house together."

"Uh." Holly seemed at a loss for words, and Gary finally came out of his stupor.

"How are my princesses? Annie, are you sure you don't want some graham crackers and milk with Eva?"

Holly's glance snapped over her shoulder at him with a look that could only be described as relief. He could well imagine the difficulty she'd have answering Annie's question without hurting his little girl's feelings.

"I was just telling Miss Holly that if you got married, she could be your queen and Eva and I your princesses."

"You already are my princesses. All of you."

"But then we could live in a big castle like Miss Sophie and Mr. Ian's house."

Gary swung his daughter in his arms and laughed. "I don't think we'd be able to afford a castle like Ian O'Connor's."

Annie squealed in delight. "Why? 'Cause you have to be on TV to have a big house like his?"

"Exactly. And I'm not on TV. Now, do you want a snack?"

"Yes, three graham crackers, please," Annie said.

"Can I have another cracker, Mr. Gary?" Eva called.

"Yes, of course."

Holly rose from the couch and followed them into the kitchen. "Yum, a graham cracker and milk would hit the spot right about now."

Annie hunkered down at the table next to Eva while the two adults went about preparing snacks for everyone.

When they were all seated, Gary couldn't help but notice how comfortable it felt to have the four of them sharing a meal like this. Holly dunked a graham square in milk and popped it into her mouth. A drop landed on her chin. Without thinking, Gary took his napkin and wiped the white bead away. Holly wiggled her brows as she chewed.

Three of the most important people sat right here, in his kitchen, and the thought of having Holly and Eva in his life permanently wasn't as scary as he would have expected. He blinked and shook away the errant notion. *It's just me and Annie, Holly doesn't want another man, and I don't need to risk another woman in my life turning into a drama queen.*

As soon as the thought popped into his head, Gary realized that title was unfair when it came to Holly. She'd proved that to him during the early days of their arrangement.

He'd come by to pick up Annie and both the girls ran out to him crying that Holly was sick. He found her balled up in the corner of her darkened bedroom, having a panic attack. His chivalrous instincts and training ran far too deep to leave her alone.

Assuring the girls everything would be fine, he sent them off to finish their dinner while he held Holly until the wheezing and shaking subsided. When she calmed down, he helped her into bed and determined to stay the night. Once the girls were bedded down, he returned to Holly's room with a cup of tea. She'd turned on the light and was sitting up with an open magazine on her lap, all signs of her freak-out gone. Her swift recovery, so different from Claire's long, drawn-out depressions, stunned him.

"I'm sorry about that," she said without looking at him. "Thanks for taking care of the girls. Is Annie staying the night?"

"Yes. So am I."

Her eyebrows winged up and she shook her head. "No need. I'll be fine." The hard determination in her eyes and resolve in her voice gave him little doubt that she would recover. Eventually.

"How long?" he asked crossing his arms.

"The panic attacks?"

He nodded.

"I used to have them back in Las Vegas. But not since I moved out here."

"What triggered it?"

She shrugged, glancing away.

He waited. Patience came with the job, and he knew that she knew what caused the attack.

Finally she sighed. "It was a letter from Omar's parents. It wasn't very nice. They're pissed they weren't able to get any sort of custody of Eva."

The detective in him moved to the forefront. "Did they threaten you?"

Her chocolate-brown eyes met his and she frowned. "Not exactly. But they certainly called me all sorts of rude and inappropriate names."

"Where's the letter?"

She picked up the magazine, studying the front cover. "I shredded it."

He ground his teeth with frustration but answered evenly. "If you get any more, don't shred them. Hand them over to me. Understand?"

The fine lines of her jaw and cheekbones were in silhouette, and the lamp played off her dark blond tresses as she nodded. It was the first time he'd felt the stirrings of inappropriate sexual feelings toward her.

He had spent that night on the couch, and to his relief, by morning that tug he'd felt in his gut had disappeared. Days passed and nothing more was said, so as far as he knew, no more letters arrived, and he'd never seen another incident like that again. Holly always seemed to remain on an even keel, especially in front of the girls.

She may have looked like a soft flower with her honey hair, slender lines, and artsy-style clothing, but she was one tough cookie underneath. Gary glanced up at Holly as she wiped cracker crumbs off Eva's face. No, it was unfair to even remotely compare Holly to his former wife's weakness. Still, he needed to remember that he was a cop with a demanding job and a child to raise. Holly was a close friend. That was it.

Chapter Three

"Look, right here in this wave, you can see how the impasto creates depth and texture." I drew my hand along the lines of the oils.

"Yes. The paint seems to be coming off the canvas, almost like a relief." Leighton removed his glasses and leaned in closer to peer at the painting. "How long did you say you've had this on display?"

"It came in Friday. I've contacted a select few clients I knew would appreciate the dramatic feel of Camponetti's work."

"Quite a coup getting this piece. It's my understanding she only displays in London and New York." He continued his study.

"You're correct." I silently gave myself a pat on the back for convincing Marcello to bid on the piece when it went up on a private auction site.

"Excuse me." Kaitlin, a student from the Art Center College of Design and part-time gallery assistant, stood on my left. "Ms. Hartland, you've got a phone call."

"Could you take a message, please? I'm with a customer," I said with a smile while silently gritting my teeth. I'd left strict instructions not to interrupt me. Leighton was a persnickety client who'd purchased a few million dollars' worth of artwork from the gallery in the past three years. The Camponetti was a potential $250,000 sale for us, and Leighton was the type to take offense if he didn't have my full attention.

"I understand, ma'am. But it's your nanny. She said it was urgent."

My eyes darted back and forth between the client and Kaitlin. Leighton continued to study the artwork from different positions.

"I apologize, Leighton. Would you mind if I …"

"Children are such a burden, aren't they?" He sighed. "Go take your call. I'm going to be here a while."

"Why don't I have Kaitlin get you something to drink? Wine, Scotch, cappuccino?" I tried to smooth over the offense.

"Perrier, in a glass, two cubes of ice."

"Right away, sir." Kaitlin scurried off to do his bidding.

"I'll only be a moment." My footsteps echoed through the gallery as I strode to my office at the front. "Hello, Sanvi."

"Hi. Listen, I'm sorry to call you at work, but there is a situation."

My stomach plummeted. "What's wrong? Are the girls okay?"

"They're fine. We're at Gary's house, and there is a woman at the door claiming to be Annie's mother. I called Gary first but couldn't get ahold of him."

My breath caught in my throat. Due to her abandonment, Gary had his ex-wife declared unfit and stripped her of all custodial rights. She knew she wasn't supposed to have contact with Annie, or should have known.

"Oh, lord. Did Annie see her?"

"No. The girls are playing in the backyard."

"Good. Don't let Claire in."

"I haven't, but she's hanging out on the front porch with a tall, blond guy."

"Okay, tell her they need to get off the property or I will call the police and have them removed. I'll try to track down Gary, and one or both of us will be home as soon as possible. Go ahead and bring the girls inside and try to keep them occupied. Keep Annie away from the front windows. If Claire drives away, take the girls out back and cut through the neighbors' yards to get to my house."

"Will do."

I hung up and called Gary's cell, but it went straight to voicemail. After leaving him a message, I tried his desk number, then contacted the detective supervisor.

"Alan Grant."

"Hi Alan, this is Holly Hartland. We met a few months ago at the annual picnic; I'm Gary Sumner's neighbor."

"I remember. What can I do for you?"

"I'm trying to track Gary down, and he's not answering his phone. Do you know where he is?"

"Let me check .... It looks like he's in court today. Is there a problem?"

"I'm afraid so. Our nanny just called to tell me that his ex-wife showed up at the house. I'm about to head home right now to deal with it. Is there any way to get a message to him?"

"I can do that. You want him to get home as soon as possible?"

"Thank you, yes. Have him give me a call when he can."

"I'm not sure when he'll be able to leave. Do you need me to send a cruiser over?"

Luckily, I didn't have to explain the situation further. The grapevine being what it was, most of the guys at the precinct had heard about Claire's shitty behavior, and typical cop style, the department rallied around its own.

"Not yet. I'll call back and let you know if the need arises."

After I hung up with the detective, I steeled myself to the possibility that I'd lose the Camponetti sale. There was no way Leighton would lower himself to deal with Kaitlin, a mere assistant. The girls needed me, and with the owners of Le Pinceau out of town, there was nothing I could do. I gave Kaitlin directions to close up the gallery at five, then braced myself to deal with Mr. Persnickety.

Leighton had pulled up a stool and sat with legs crossed, staring at the piece.

"So, what do you think?" I asked him.

"It's beguiling. I can't take my eyes off it."

"I'm sorry to do this, but I've had a bit of an emergency come up and I'm going to have to leave you. If you decide you want the piece, simply give me a call, and I'll arrange for the payment and delivery."

Leighton finally pulled his eyes away from the painting to tune in on me. "Who else are you showing it to?"

"Lori Dunne is coming by tomorrow." Actually, I hadn't yet arranged for other clients to view the piece, but I knew that Leighton—in his head— had created a completely one-sided rivalry with Lori, and I shamelessly used this knowledge to my advantage.

"Cancel her appointment. I'll take it. Can you get it delivered by Monday?"

"Of course. I'll get the paperwork started and have it for you to sign tomorrow. In the meantime, if you need anything else, just ask Kaitlin."

I rarely pitted clients against each other, because I never knew when it might come back and bite me in the ass. Today it paid off and allowed me to get out quickly, but as I drove toward Gary's house, I swore never to do it again with Leighton.

It normally took thirty minutes to get home from work; I made it in twenty. On the way over, Sanvi texted that she'd moved the children back to my place. When I arrived at Gary's, I didn't see any unusual cars or strangers hanging around the house, so I drove home. The front door was locked and I keyed in.

"Sanvi?"

"We're in the kitchen."

I found the girls watching the nanny as she heated milk on the stove.

"Mommy, you're home early." Eva clapped and bounced in her seat.

I hugged and kissed both the girls. "I am. It was a slow day, so I thought I'd come home and spend time with you girls. What are we having?"

"Hot chocolate. Would you like some?" Sanvi asked. Even though she seemed calm on the outside, I could see that her hand shook as she laid the spoon down.

"That sounds delicious but, no, thank you."

The girls chatted to me about their day as Sanvi finished preparing the hot chocolate and passed out some Teddy Grahams for their snack. Once the girls tucked into their food, Sanvi and I subtly left the kitchen to speak privately.

"Did you find Gary?"

"He's in court today. No word on when he'll be out." I explained my conversation with the supervising detective. "What happened with Claire?"

"After I told her that if she didn't leave we'd call the police, she and her boyfriend got in their car and tore off down the road."

My phone dinged, revealing a text from Gary.

I'll be home in half an hour. Where are you?

Everyone is at my house now.

"Gary's on his way. Sanvi, can you stay until he gets here?" I could have let her go home, but I found comfort in having her remain until Gary arrived.

"Of course, I can stay as long as you need."

We were sculpting Play-Doh with the girls in the kitchen when the doorbell rang.

"I'll get that," I said, motioning for Sanvi to remain with the kids.

Expecting Gary, I didn't check out the window before opening the door. I knew the moment I laid eyes on her who stood on the other side of my screen. I'd never met Claire, but I'd seen a photo of her in Annie's room. Even though the brown hair had been dyed blond, the round face and striking blue eyes were unmistakable. I slipped out the door, closing it behind me.

"What are you doing here?" I spotted a black Porsche Boxster down the street and could barely make out a blond head sitting behind the wheel.

"I saw you pulling out of Gary's driveway and recognized you. Your sister was the one who got shot last year. Right?"

"You can't be here."

"Is she in there?"

"Claire, you can't be here."

"Are you and Gary sleeping together?"

"You need to leave. Now." I kept glancing between her and the Porsche. Luckily, the driver remained in the car. If he made a move, I'd be on the phone faster than a jackrabbit on speed, and I'd tell Alan to send in the SWAT team.

"I didn't mean any offense. You seem like a nice person. I just want to see my daughter."

"I'm sorry, you can't."

"You're a mother, right? Mom-to-mom, you understand. Can't I just see her for a moment?" Her eyes shone with unshed tears and her lip trembled.

"Claire, you know the rules. You signed the paperwork."

"It doesn't count. I was off my meds."

"I'm sorry; it's not happening."

"I didn't know what I was doing." She wrung her hands and spoke in wheedling voice.

My eyes flared. "Did you know what you were doing when you left her in the middle of the night with a sixteen-year-old babysitter and a Dear John letter on the mantel?"

She winced as though I'd slapped her. "I just want to see her for a few minutes. It's Christmastime and I need to tell her that I'm okay. Oh, and that I love her." She said the last sentence as an afterthought.

"No."

"She'll want to hear about my travels, where I've been. Gary doesn't need to know," she leaned in and whispered.

This woman is unbelievable. "What then?" I crossed my arms. "You'll be on your merry way, off to the next adventure. How do you think that'll make Annie feel, with you bopping in and out of her life when it's convenient for you?"

"I'm her mother, damn it, and I want to see her." Her confidential wheedling changed in an instant, and she pounded her fist into her palm as she spoke. "I gave birth to her. It's my right as her mother."

"This is exactly why you don't have rights. You see, Claire, when we have children, we have to stop thinking about ourselves and put our children's needs above our own." My hushed tones didn't eradicate any of the ire or censure from my statement.

Her eyes flashed and her face turned crimson. She opened her mouth, but before she could utter a word, Gary's unmarked cruiser, with lights flashing, pulled into the driveway. Claire's face drained of color.

"Claire, what are you doing? You don't belong here," he said as he stepped out of the vehicle.

"Oh, darling, it's been so long. You look so handsome in that suit." She minced up to him in her four-inch heels and placed her perfectly manicured hands on his chest.

Ugh. What a faker!

"I thought we could sit down and talk. Maybe over a cup of coffee?" she cooed.

Behind Gary, a sunglass-wearing, blond behemoth unfolded himself from the Porsche, and I jerked forward, making a sound in the back of my throat that sounded like an injured cow. Claire must have seen it too; her posture stiffened and her black talons clutched Gary's lapels. Instantly, he spun around, detaching Claire as he went, pushed his jacket aside, and placed his hand on the weapon at his hip.

The blonde's long legs quickly ate up the pavement, and he stopped at the end of the driveway. His jeans conformed to his muscular thighs, and his tight, black polo barely allowed enough room for his thick neck. My stomach churned and I stood frozen in fear.

"Liebling, ve need to go. You said ten minutes. Stefan is vaiting for us." The Thor-like creature spoke with a European accent I couldn't pinpoint.

"Yes, darling. I'm almost finished. I just need a tiny moment. Why don't you be a sweetheart and pull the car up?"

He looked between the three of us, undecided.

"*Gehen sie auf, die Liebe. Ich bin gleich da. Bitte,*" Go on, love. I'll be there soon, Claire said in a cajoling voice. Thor shrugged his linebacker shoulders and returned to the sports car. I didn't relax, and Gary didn't take his eyes off him until the door closed

"Dare I ask?" He turned to Claire with a raised brow.

"Cristos."

"I'm to assume Viktor is out of the picture?" Gary pronounced it Veek-toor.

Claire shrugged. The Porsche rolled to a stop at the curb.

"Leave now and I won't arrest you, Claire." His eyes remained hard and emotionless.

She gasped. "You wouldn't dare."

"In a heartbeat. Get off Holly's property and don't return. There will be no coffee, no dinner, no lunch, no nothing. Go. Now."

With a huff, she strode across my lawn. Thor pushed the car door open from inside and she climbed in, slamming it behind her. The window silently slid down, and she left us with a cliché parting shot before the car peeled out. "You'll be hearing from my lawyer."

"Yeah, you do that," he muttered under his breath.

Once the car turned the corner, my legs gave out and I plopped down onto the brick walkway, dropping my head into my hands.

Gary's black wingtips strode into my line of vision, and he crouched down to my level. "Are you okay?"

Warm fingers gripped my shoulder. I nodded.

"I'm sorry; I didn't think she would have the nerve to show her face."

I started to shake.

"Hey, hey, what's this? It's okay; they're gone. You and the girls are safe."

I pulled my head out of my hands and allowed the giggles to erupt. "Did you see that guy? He looked like a cartoon character or something. *Liebling*, Stefan is vaiting," I imitated, brushing away a tear. "I felt like I was in a soap opera."

Gary sat on the ground next to me. "That's what my life was like." He ran his hand through his hair. "What the hell am I going to do about her?"

"Restraining order?"

"I don't believe she's a danger to anyone. She's not vindictive. Just flighty and self-involved. I suppose I'll talk to the lawyer and see what he has to say. The sad thing is, I suspect something else will soon come along to distract her, and she'll be off into the sunset."

"We'll have to figure it out what to do in the meantime. Poor Sanvi, she probably had a minor heart attack."

"You're right. How are the girls?"

"Oblivious, as far as I can tell." I tapped a finger against my chin. "Maybe I can ask Sophie if I can borrow Sirius for a while."

Gary threw back his head and let out a belly laugh.

"What? What's so funny?"

"That's not a bad idea. Claire has allergies and absolutely abhors dogs. Sirius is such a big lug, the moment she set eyes on him, she'd run screaming from the house. I can just picture it in my head."

I, too, pictured her scuttling down the driveway in her stilettos, screeching like an angry peacock. The image had me giggling, again. "How on earth could you marry someone who didn't like dogs?"

"I didn't find out until too late." He sheepishly looked away.

I placed a hand on his shoulder. "Seriously, how did she draw you in?"

Gary's eyes focused on the distance. "Claire could be ... charming and wickedly funny when she was up. When we met, she was on a high, a ball full of energy. She offset my dour countenance and made me smile."

"You're not dour."

"We only dated a few months before getting married. At first I thought her depressions were just her being dramatic, vying for attention, because they didn't last very long and often commenced after an argument. After Annie was born, things changed. She suffered from postpartum depression and was hospitalized. That's when we realized she had already been suffering. When she was on medication, she leveled out and life was normal. But I worked late or got called in and she had to hold down the fort. Responsibility didn't sit well on her shoulders."

"And she blamed you."

"She'd 'forget' to take her meds if I wasn't around to remind her."

I was about to say something about having poor taste in women, but I snapped my trap shut before voicing the comment. After all, I married an abuser—people in glass houses and all that.

"Hell." Gary rose and held a hand out to me. "Let's check on the girls."

"It's not your fault, you know." Gary always seemed to take the weight of the world on his shoulders. Some would say it was the cop in him, but I had a feeling no matter what his profession, he would have that instinctive need to accept responsibilities that weren't necessarily his own.

"Alley-oop." His hand clamped around mine and he pulled me to my feet. An unexpected jolt zoomed through my system. I stared at Gary's lapels, pretending to ignore what the closeness of his body did to me. He must not have noticed, because he turned away without comment and reached for the door. As he did so, I caught sight of the gun at his hip.

When we started this nanny-sharing arrangement, Gary and I had a discussion about the department-issued, .40 caliber Sig Sauer and the precautions he took to keep the children safe. When not on his body, it along with his mace and two private weapons were locked in a touchpad safe in his bedroom. The weapon still gave me pause, but no longer instilled heart-pounding fear as it did when I arrived in California. Gary wanted to bring me out to the range so I could learn how to handle a weapon myself, but I had yet to take him up on his offer. Right now, our safety relied on the top-of-the-line home security system my sister installed last year and the Louisville Slugger under my bed, also a gift from Sophie. She said it was a lucky bat, and indeed, from what I understood, it had saved her life last year when my ex-husband came looking for me and held her at gunpoint.

Oblivious to my tumbling thoughts, Gary held the door for me, absently gazing past my shoulder. This was turning out to be a very strange day, indeed.

Chapter Four

The chime of the bell set Sirius a-barking and made me stride to the front door to help Sophie and the caterers bring in the food.

"Sirius, *sit!*" Sophie ordered. "Holly, can you put him upstairs in the study?"

"I'm on it."

Last week, Ian had decided to host a "small holiday gathering" for the cast and crew of his show, *LA Heat*. The guest list ballooned to well over a hundred, and my sister begged Poppy for help. Due to Poppy's own busy holiday party schedule, she and Adam had only been able to take a long weekend for their honeymoon and planned to head to Tahiti after the new year. She called in a favor for Sophie and found a catering company willing to squeeze the party into their calendar. I personally owed my sister so many favors I'd lost count. When she asked, there was no way I could turn her down.

Given that Gary had been unable to attend Poppy's wedding, I'd arranged a babysitter for tonight so he could come. It had been five days since the Claire incident, and we'd neither seen nor heard anything further from her. Gary figured she'd already moved on to her next escapade; I had a gut feeling we hadn't seen the last of her.

An hour later, the house hummed with guests and Sophie's "little" get-together filled every room, spilling out onto the back patio. The huge dining table glittered beneath the beautiful glass chandelier, with an elegant mix of finger foods, meat dishes, and a glorious tower of petit fours gracing the center. Four bartenders, two in the kitchen and two outside on the patio, mixed drinks and poured wine for the hundred-plus partygoers. Cars lined the street, and Ian's hired security managed the traffic and paparazzi. The guests were a mix between Ian's Hollywood crowd and Sophie's vendors and contracting crew.

The party had been in full swing for an hour, and Gary had yet to arrive. I texted

Where are you?

Closed a big case today. Need to finish wrapping the report. Should be there in 30 mins. Sorry. Meant to call. Got distracted.

Okay. You better not bail on me. Soph picked me up, so you're my ride home.

Be there soon. Promise.

For some unknown reason, his lateness made me edgy. Absently, I watched the bartender shake up a martini, and my party mood flattened. Obviously, as a detective, the job came first, but I'd been looking forward to spending time with him in an adult setting—no kids. Poppy was right, I'd never seen Gary "let down his hair," and Sophie's party was an excellent excuse to allow the two of us to escape our daily cares for a few hours. I'd even gone so far as to purchase a shimmery new blouse for the gathering. A burst of laughter from behind interrupted my brooding. Around me groups chatted, bartenders popped open bottles of beer and uncorked wine, Sophie's beautiful Christmas tree glittered, and music thumped in the background. *What am I thinking?* I gave myself a mental head slap. Why was I allowing Gary's lateness to get to me? *It's not like we're on a date. It's just Gary. He'll get here when he gets here. Enough.*

I picked up my glass of wine, surveyed the crowd, and headed into the fray. Twenty minutes later, after getting hit on by Sophie's flooring supplier, a crew member from *LA Heat,* and a masonry specialist, I needed a break and escaped to the bathroom. Both of the main level toilets were in use, so I headed upstairs.

Light shone through the cracked door, and as I knocked, it swung open, revealing a dark head bent over the counter sniffing the last bits of, what I assumed to be, cocaine with a rolled up twenty.

"Excuse me."

The head popped up. "Hey, doll face, just finishing up in here." Wide, bloodshot eyes darted around as he wiped the powder from his nose and pocketed the money. Then he surreptitiously dusted the remains of the drugs off the countertop and licked it from his finger.

Eww. My arms crossed, and I gave him the evil-eye glare. "I think you need to leave. *Now.*"

"It's all good. On my way, on my way. I'm finished here."

His lanky frame slid past, and a cloud of Drakkar cologne overwhelmed me. I covered my nose and a hand smacked my butt. I gritted my teeth and held back my inclination to slap the self-satisfied smile off his face as he bounced down the hall in a drug-induced buzz.

Sophie and Ian were not going to be happy when I told them about the coke-snorter in their bathroom. Neither tolerated drugs. After using the facilities, I found disinfectant under the sink and wiped down the counter before returning to the party.

My eyes searched the great room, and sure enough, coke-snorter hovered in a corner, over a petite blonde, speaking quickly and using effusive hand gestures. She nodded and seemed to be fascinated by his conversation. Neither Sophie nor Ian could be found inside, so I worked my way through the crowd out to the back patio, which was lit up by outdoor heaters, a fire pit, and little fairy lights that had been strung around the fruit trees and shrubs. Light jackets and heaters kept everyone warm enough, in the mild California evening breeze.

Sophie and Ian snuggled together on a lounger, laughing and chatting with a group of folks. Their bodies spoke the secret language of love. Both exchanged constant eye contact, and their smiling countenances simply sparkled, making the pair stand out among the crowd.

I gulped down the dread of ruining the party for them and decided to go directly to the security guys instead and tell them about the cokehead.

Sophie spotted me.

"Holly!" Her hand waved me over. "Join us."

I vacillated for a moment, but Poppy, who must have recently arrived, turned her head and gestured me over, too. A dozen people sat in various chairs grouped around the crackling fire pit.

Ian turned to a guy sitting on his right. "Hey, mate, move over and give Holly your seat."

The dark-haired, Greek godlike creature rose and with a perfect smile offered me his seat.

I was pretty sure the guy had been in a popular car chase film, but I waved him off. "No, I was just checking to see how things were going out here. You want me to bring out some goodies to munch on?"

"Forget it, Holly. Take a load off. You've done enough today. Sit. Mario doesn't mind, do you?" Sophie directed a smile at the Greek god.

"Anything for Ian's beautiful fiancé." Mario scooped up Sophie's hand and kissed it.

She giggled.

"Here now, you tosser. Leave my lady alone. Go make love to Holly. She's available," Ian chided.

Mario's teeth flashed, and he gave me a look that could only be described as … smoldering. He delivered it so quickly and perfectly, I was pretty sure he'd worked on it in the mirror, which kind of ruined the effect.

"Sorry, Mario. Holly's crossed actors off the list," Sophie piped in.

He slapped a hand to his heart, and the smoldering look turned into puppy dog eyes. "My fair lady, say it isn't true. You wouldn't discriminate against my race."

"It's not you. It's the litter of paparazzi you tend to drag along in your wake that I don't care for." I shifted my stance and glanced over my shoulder to see if the druggie still remained in his corner with the blonde, but they were out of my view.

"They never follow me," Mario denied vehemently.

I rolled my eyes and waved him back to his seat. "Save it. Soph, I've got to check on something then I'll be back."

My boot heels clip-clopped against the concrete as I scurried my way through the crowd toward the house, but I didn't get any farther than the back door before a gentle hand on my shoulder stopped me.

"What's wrong?"

Sophie knew me too well. Something in my body language must have given me away.

"Umm." My eyes darted around as I debated telling her the situation. I glanced over her shoulder and found Ian's intense stare on the two of us and gave in. In a low voice I explained, "Okay, I went upstairs to your bathroom because the two down here were occupied, and I found a guy snorting coke."

Sophie's brows knit. "In the master bath?"

"No, the guest bath."

"What the hell?" Her voice rose an octave, and she planted her hands on hips.

"I decided not to bother you and Ian with this and was about to tell someone on the security team to remove him."

She pinched her lower lip and nodded. "You might be right. I'll go with you to get security."

"What's up?" Ian came up behind Sophie and gripped her shoulder.

Her eyes flew to him, and I could see the debate war across her features before she sighed. "Holly just found some guy snorting coke in our bathroom."

Ian's frowning gaze turned to me.

I grimaced and nodded.

"I think I saw Ziggy on the far side of the pool. Can you ask him to come here, luv, while I have Holly point the fellow out to me?"

"Good idea." Sophie slipped around Ian's large frame.

"So, where is this wanker?"

"Last time I saw him, he was in the corner right over there." We shifted into the living room until he came into sight. "See the short blonde in the blue dress? It's the skinny guy wearing the sunglasses."

A large presence joined the pair of us. Ziggy, a friend of Ian's who provided private investigation and bodyguard services, stood on my right. Ian hired Ziggy to watch over me and Eva last year during the insane-killer-husband incident. He had the width and girth of a professional sumo wrestler, or prehistoric dinosaur, depending on which way you looked at it. Either way, the cokehead didn't stand a chance with both Ian and Ziggy coming his way.

Poppy joined Sophie and me as we watched the two men approach him.

"What's going on?" she asked.

"Holly found that skinny guy in the black shirt snorting coke in my bathroom." Sophie indicated with her chin.

The three of us stood in a row, arms crossed, as the party went on around us, watching Ian speak to the offender. It seemed as though he and Ziggy were trying to remain low-key to get the guy to leave. Unfortunately, people high on coke weren't usually docile.

"Too bad Gary's not here. He could take care of this," Poppy said.

"He's working late to finish up some paperwork. He should be …" As if he was conjured by my words, Gary walked into my line of sight, and both a thrill of delight along with relief swept over me. *Speak of the devil.*

• • •

In view of the fact that he still wore his service weapon, Gary declined the coat check lady's offer to take his navy blazer. He loosened his tie and shoved it into a pocket as he worked his way through the clumps of eclectic partygoers. End-of-the-week fatigue had set in, and he would have preferred to go directly home. On the whole, big parties weren't his thing, but he'd promised Holly he would stop by and he didn't want to let her down. He stepped into the great room, searching the crowd for a familiar face.

"What the fuck, man! Who told you that?" On alert, Gary's head whipped to his right to find a tall, skinny guy shake Ian's hand off his shoulder.

Ian said something, but Gary couldn't hear what the altercation was about over the din of the party. A blond woman started speaking quickly to skinny man and tugged at his sleeve.

The skinny guy shook his hand free from her grip. "Forget that! I'm not leaving. The party's just getting star-ted!" He swung his hand in a grand gesture that caught her on the chin and snapped her head back.

Gary weaved through the throng to get to the group, but people kept stepping in his way and he couldn't see what was happening. Then a hush fell over the party and he heard Ian say, "Time to leave, you wank biscuit."

Gary pushed his way through a pair of black-haired ladies with tattooed arm sleeves and found the guy folded in half, holding his gut.

"What's going on?" he asked.

Ziggy and Ian helped the wheezing guy upright. His sunglasses had fallen off, and Gary instantly recognized that look—red, watery eyes, dilated pupils.

"Just helping a party crasher out the door. No big deal," Ziggy said.

Adam thrust through the crowd and went immediately to the blond girl, who must have bitten her lip or tongue, because she had tears in her eyes and the hand at her mouth had blood on the fingers.

"Come with me, miss. I'm a doctor. I can help you with that." Guests parted and he steered her away from the group.

"Need some help, guys?" Gary asked his host.

"No thanks, detective. Ziggy and I will just escort this tosser off the premises."

The boys got about two steps away when the cokehead shook Ian off, turned, and pointed at someone across the room. "I know you snitched! I'm gonna get you, bitch!"

Everyone, including Gary, followed his finger to find Holly standing immobilized with a pale face and wide, deer-in-headlights eyes. Poppy and Sophie stood guard on either side; both ladies slid their arms across her shoulders and closed ranks.

Holly's frightened gaze locked with Gary's and raw anger blazed through him. His hand fisted. Before he could turn to use it, there was an "oof" and a sound of flesh meeting flesh. Gary tore his eyes from Holly to find Ian shaking his wrist and the cokehead holding a hand to his nose. A couple of wiseacres clapped and whistled. Two guys wearing black cargo pants and black T-shirts with the word SECURITY across the back came onto the scene. They, along with Ziggy, escorted the unwelcome guest out the door.

Ian stood, arms crossed, and watched them leave. "Bugger. I can just see the Internet headlines. This'll be trending on Twitter and end up on the *Today* show by morning. Sophie's going to hate that."

"The guy's high on something. I should arrest him."

"Nah. Relax, detective; Ziggy will take care of it."

Gary strained at the bit to get over to comfort Holly, but duty kept him from leaving Ian's side. "I have to ask, do you know of anyone selling drugs here?"

"They bloody well better not." Ian turned to the crowd and bellowed, "Hey, you lot, if anyone else is planning to snort, shoot, swallow, or smoke something illegal, you'd better get the hell out of my house. I don't put up with wankers on dope. If I see any, I'll have the copper here run you in. You got me?" He hooked a thumb at Gary.

The crowd nodded, a few mumbled "yes," one guy shouted, "you tell 'em Officer McKay."

Ian muttered some sort of British profanity that went over Gary's head.

"Let me know if you need anything else," he said.

"I'm good, mate. But you could use a pint. Let me get you one."

"In a minute. I want to check on Holly." Holly's honey mane wasn't visible through the crowd, but Gary spotted Poppy's red locks and headed in that direction. The upbeat party mood that pulsed through the room when he arrived had become subdued. People spoke in low voices, and a number of souls drifted out back. He found Holly being comforted by Poppy, Sophie, and a few other strangers.

"Don't worry, doll, he's some coked-up loser who won't remember his own name tomorrow, much less who was at the party tonight." Poppy rubbed Holly's back in a reassuring manner.

Not wanting to worry Holly further, he didn't bother to contradict Poppy's incorrect assumption. Since coke was an upper, users remembered things quite clearly the next morning.

Holly frowned and looked uncomfortable.

"Holly." Gary reached for her, and Poppy moved aside to allow him into the circle.

Her face transformed. The V between her brows relaxed, and before he knew it, she'd wrapped her silk-covered arms around him and buried her face in his neck.

"Gary," she breathed.

He enfolded her warm body and drank in her citrus perfume. Her hug, though not unwelcome, surprised him. He expected Holly to have held tightly to her sister, and it pleased him that she sought comfort in his embrace. However, he also knew from police work that people did unusual things in emotional situations, and it wouldn't have been the first time a distraught woman turned to him for human comfort. "It's okay. He's gone."

She nodded. The circle of people dispersed, leaving only Poppy and Sophie behind.

"Thank god you came. I saw you arrive. Is Ian okay? What about that girl who got hit?" Holly asked.

"Adam is taking care of her." He rubbed her back.

"Poor thing; I felt for her."

"Do you know who she is?"

She shook her head, keeping her face snuggled against his neck. "Never seen either of them before."

"Soph, you and Ian know how to throw a fun party." They looked over their shoulders to find a tall, dark-haired man swilling a bottle of beer.

"Thanks, Mario. We try." Sophie gave a halfhearted smile.

"It's time we get things back on track. Leave it to me." He winked and elbowed past them. "Okay, folks, the show is over." Mario strut into the crowd. "Who wants to see my party trick?"

A dozen hands waved in the air and a drunken female called out, "I'd like to see your party dick."

Mario pointed at a pair of girls leaning against the wall. "Stand back, ladies."

They moved away. In an instant, Mario ran at the wall, climbed halfway up, and back flipped to a round of cheers. The mood in the room seemed to lighten—someone turned the music up, and the conversation noise increased.

"I suppose that'll take their minds off this debacle," Sophie mumbled.

Poppy shook her head and gave an eye roll. "I need a drink after that."

"Me, too. Holly, are you going to be all right?"

Holly pulled out of Gary's embrace. "Yeah. I'm fine. We'll join you in a minute."

"Save you a seat." Sophie followed Poppy out the back door.

"Sorry you got dragged into that." She looked sheepishly at him from beneath her lashes.

"It's nothing." Though Holly seemed to have relaxed, he watched for signs that might bring on a panic attack. "Why did that guy have a beef with you?"

"I found him snorting a line of coke in the bathroom and ratted him out."

"Jesus, I wish you hadn't told me that." Gary ran a hand through his hair.

"I'm sure he brought it himself. You heard Ian; he doesn't put up with drugs. I don't think anyone would dare try to deal here."

"Let's hope you're right."

"I'm right. If you don't mind, I think I need to get loaded. Feel free to join me. We'll catch a cab home."

He gazed at her, taking in the tight skirt and the sexy blouse that exposed a hint of cleavage. "You drink. I'll drive us home."

"Suit yourself. C'mon." She tugged his hand and towed him out to the back patio.

They slid into a pair of vacant stools at the outdoor kitchen that was pulling duty as tonight's bar. Holly smacked her hand on the granite counter and barked, "I'll have a shot of tequila."

The bartender, a young twenty-something with nose and eyebrow piercings, expertly poured a shot in a lowball glass. Gary noted the slight tremor in Holly's hand as she scooped it up and slung the liquor back in one gulp. Her face twisted into the scrunchy, tequila-shot face. She waved off the lime chaser and smacked her lips.

"Want another?" The bartender smirked.

Wiping her mouth with the back of her hand, she shook her head. "I'll have whatever they're having." She indicated the wine glasses in front of Sophie and Poppy.

"What about you?" he asked Gary.

"Club soda with a lime."

"I heard some coked-up dude's got it in for you," the bartender said as he poured the drinks.

Gary gritted his teeth, clenched his fist, and counted backward from ten to keep from reaching across the bar to shake this insensitive prick.

Poppy sniffed. "Him? I wouldn't be afraid of a twerp like that. I once had a bridezilla threaten to rip my nipples off with a pair of ice-cube tongs and shove them up my cooch if I didn't get her wedding dress zipped up all the way."

Sophie choked and put a hand over her mouth. Giggling, Holly whacked her sister on the back as the bartender passed Sophie a napkin.

She blew her nose and dabbed at her watering eyes. "Omigod. You just made me snort wine through my nose. Ow, that burns."

"So what happened with the bride?" Gary asked, grateful to Poppy for changing the atmosphere.

"It was her fault." Poppy shrugged. "She gained, like, ten pounds stress eating in the two weeks leading up to the wedding.

I swear every time I saw her, she was shoveling something into her cake-hole. So, I strapped her into an industrial grade corset, which she'd sworn she wouldn't need to wear, and zipped that puppy closed. Her boobs squished out the side like a jelly donut."

"I'll have a Guinness, mate." Ian wrapped an arm around Sophie's waist.

"How's the blonde who got hit on the chin?" Sophie asked.

"Daniella? She's one of the make-up artists. She'll be all right. Adam has everything in hand. Pip of a fellow you married there, Poppy. I'm chuffed we've got a doctor in the group."

"Gee, Ian, I'm glad to know he meets with your approval. Because I sure wouldn't want to marry someone you disapproved of."

"Smart-arse," Ian mumbled before taking a swig of beer.

Gary watched the easy banter between the Holly's friends and envied their camaraderie. Whether because of his training, or innate personality, he lacked the witty charisma that seemed to define this troupe. Though they'd always been welcoming, he often felt like an outsider looking in. It had never bothered him in the past, but for some reason it did tonight. Looking from Poppy to Ian to Holly, he determined to make tonight different and went about making himself a part of the group rather than allowing his usual reserved demeanor to keep him aloof.

• • •

Just past midnight, Gary opened the passenger door to a gently snoring Holly. He'd paid and sent the sitter home and now had the task of getting his lovely but abundantly inebriated neighbor into the house.

"Holly." He shook her shoulder. "Haa-lleee. *Holly!* Wake up." Nothing. He stood back.

I could just throw a blanket on her and leave her in the car overnight. He scrubbed his eyes. *No. What would the neighbors think?*

He reached across to unbuckle the seat belt, and as he did so, his arm brushed up against her soft breast. She sighed and shifted. He froze. The snoring started up again. Gary rotated Holly's legs around outside of the car door and put her booted feet on the ground. Her silky shirt made her slide effortlessly to the left so that she lay sprawled across the seat with her pencil skirt slipped above her knees. Gary took only a moment to enjoy the sight before leaning in to pull her torso forward onto his shoulder and out of the car. He heaved her up fireman style and closed the car door behind him with a kick. He wrestled with the storm door/ front door combination before making it into the foyer without knocking her head.

The dim glow of a nightlight shed enough illumination to navigate to her room, and Gary unfolded her onto the bed. He unzipped the boots, leaving them on the floor. Her glossy locks splayed across the comforter, and her skirt had bunched up enough to reveal the tops of her thigh-high stockings. *Damn, even three sheets to the wind she is beautiful.* Gary was not unaffected. Her perfume still clung to his shirt, and the hunger he'd been fighting all night bloomed into full-blown desire. Reluctantly, he shook away his debauched thoughts, threw a blanket over her, and left the room.

He debated spending the night on the couch, but he needed the comforts of his own bed. He also needed to get his head on straight, and that necessitated removing himself from Holly's radius.

Throughout the night, Holly had drunk steadily, ignoring the few times Gary suggested she slow down. She laughed and joked, becoming more gregarious as the night wore on. It was a side of her he'd never seen. One thing she continued to do was remain glued to his side, going so far as to hold his hand, wrap her arm around him, and on occasion run a hand up his thigh, squeezing it for emphasis at times. She'd never behaved in this manner toward him, and he attributed it to the earlier debacle and increased alcohol. But her inebriated condition aside, Gary's sexual and emotional feelings were running on the verge, and they'd both benefit from a little distance. He checked on the two sleeping girls and then locked the door behind himself as he left.

Chapter Five

Nature's needs, and a bunch of reindeer tap dancing in my head, woke me at six in the morning. After driving the porcelain bus, I downed some aspirin with a glass of water and changed out of last night's clothes. Returning to bed, I allowed my mind to dredge up what it could remember of the party. The scent of Gary's sandalwood aftershave lingered on the blouse I'd worn. I recalled throwing myself into his arms for comfort after the disturbing cokehead incident, an act that could be explained away and one that didn't seem to bother him. Then there were some shots, and that's where things got a bit hazy. I groaned as a flash of memory popped in—me leaning all over Gary, practically climbing into his lap, my hand running up his thigh.

Crap! Crap! Crap! I scrunched my eyes tight, but the recollection floated across my visual cortex. I strained the memory banks to see if there was an equally embarrassing kiss involved, but it remained a blank. No memory of getting home. Considering I was still dressed in the party outfit when I awoke, I had a bad feeling Gary might have carried me to bed.

Good lord. I drew a hand down my face. *I will never ever do tequila shots again. What must Gary think? I am a bad person. I'll have to call Sophie to find out how bad it was.*

Noise from Eva's room escalated enough to drag me from my self-castigation. The hangover limited my inclination to make a fancy meal; their breakfast consisted of cold cereal with bananas. Nobody complained. After they finished, I plopped them in front of the television with a box of crayons and stack of coloring books. Luckily, both kept the two girls entertained and quiet.

Are the girls up? I need to get Annie.

Anytime. Girls are fed and awake.

I responded to Gary's text and sipped my second cup of coffee.

Gary's car pulled into the driveway, and I met him at the door before he could ring the bell.

A small smile played around his lips as he took in my bedraggled appearance and bloodshot eyes. "How's the hangover?"

"A special treat. Thanks for asking." I winced as the sun came out from behind a cloud. "Come in. The girls are coloring."

"Daddeee!" Annie ran into Gary's arms.

"Mister Garee!"

I covered my ears as the girls happily chattered at the top of their voices, telling Gary about their night with the babysitter. He crouched to their level and asked all the appropriate questions.

"Okay, Annie, go get your backpack. Make sure you've got your Mr. Pickles," he said, referring to her purple rhinoceros, a favored stuffed animal.

The girls obediently trotted out. Gary stood, hands on hips, as his tolerant, loving gaze followed them down the hall. Then he turned to me; his eyes shuttered and his face turned neutral. I always considered it his "cop look." I had no idea what he was thinking, and it probably came in handy when questioning suspects.

Embarrassment had my cheeks burning red-hot. "Listen, I'm … uh … real sorry about my behavior last night. I don't usually drink that much and … uh … you know."

"Pass out."

"Yeah, that too."

"Too?" His brows creased. "Did I miss something?"

"No, I just meant, I don't usually, um … shit," I muttered.

"Shit?"

"I don't usually paw my neighbors," I blurted.

"Ah." His brow cleared and that small smile played around his lips again. "Don't worry. I suspect the events leading up to the bender were rather traumatic for you."

"Yes, that's it exactly." I relaxed. "That guy freaked me out. Anyway, thanks for driving me home. I don't really remember getting to bed …" I stared into the half-full mug of coffee as I ran a finger around the top of the cup.

"No, I don't suppose you would …"

"I'm ready to go, Daddy." Annie scampered into the living room and dropped her backpack at Gary's feet.

"Okay, princess, let's head out." He stroked her head.

Annie didn't need to be told twice. She skipped passed me and out the front door.

Gary scooped up the backpack and followed her, pausing in the doorway. "By the way, those were some sexy thigh highs you were wearing." He winked.

Mortification burned through me as the door shut with a thump. *Omigod, Omigod! What the hell was I doing showing him my stockings? Did that happen at the party? I've got to call Sophie.*

"Mommy, can you play with me?" Eva stood forlorn in the hallway, deflated that her friend had left, her favorite bunny hanging limply in her hand, its ears dragging on the ground.

My poor baby. "I have an even better idea. Let's get dressed and go Christmas shopping. There are only ten more days until Santa comes, and you haven't told him what you want. How will he know what to bring you?"

Her face brightened. "I want a Frozen Castle."

The call to Sophie would have to wait. "We'll visit Santa today and you can tell him. Okay?"

She took my hand as we headed back to her room, chattering about her latest favorite Disney princess.

•••

It was an exhausting day fighting the crowds and entertaining Eva as we stood in the long lines. Every year I swore to start my shopping earlier. Somehow, it never seemed to come to fruition. It wasn't until after I'd put Eva to bed that I had a chance to call my sister.

"What's up, girl? How's the hangover?" Her cheerful voice chirped across the phone lines.

"Better now, hideous this morning."

"I'm not surprised. You did that tequila shot, then at least two Jägermeister shots with Mario. Ick. On top of the shots, you threw back a few glasses of wine."

"Jesus, why didn't you stop me?"

"I tried. You weren't listening to anyone, so Gary and I started dumping your drinks. When that didn't work, I had the bartenders water them down."

"So, basically you're saying I made an ass of myself at your party."

"No, I wouldn't put it that way, exactly."

"What way *exactly* would you put it?"

"Well actually, you were pretty funny. You went on this rant about reality TV that put the group in stitches. I thought Poppy was going to pee her pants."

"What about me and Gary?"

"Yeah, that was interesting. He was in rare form, much more talkative than I've ever seen. What's going on there? Are you two doing the horizontal tango or what?"

"*Soph.* What exactly happened at the party?"

"So you're not doing the mambo-mambo?"

I moaned

"Okay, okay. You were pretty much glued at the hip all night."

"In other words, I hung all over him like bark on a tree."

"Hmm … actually, it looked mutual. You certainly hung on him, but he reciprocated. I saw his arm wrapped around your waist. And he didn't seem to *mind* you running your hand up his leg."

"Omigod." I dropped my forehead into my hand.

"Ian and I thought it was pretty cool. You two are perfect for each other. Single parents, adorable girls …"

"Uh, did I flash him my panties at your party?"

"*Eww.* Not that I saw. Did you take him to the bathroom or something?"

"Not that I can recall. But he made a comment about my thigh highs."

"Maybe your skirt rode up in the car. He and Ian practically poured you into Gary's Camry. I wouldn't be surprised if your clothes were a bit … askew."

My entire brain was a bit askew last night. "I don't remember getting home. Was I conscious?"

"When you left. But it's almost half an hour back to the house. It wouldn't surprise me if you passed out on the way."

"I was afraid of that. When I woke this morning, my boots were off, but my clothes were still on and tangled around me."

"He probably had to carry you into the house. You're lucky. I would have left your ass passed out in the car."

"Do you think he peeked at the goods while I was down for the count?" I couldn't decide if I'd be upset or flattered by Gary taking a peek.

"Hmm … no. This is Gary we're talking about. He's a Boy Scout and a good guy. I didn't see a sip of alcohol pass his lips. I can't imagine him taking advantage of a comatose woman. Much less someone as enmeshed in his life as you are."

"You're right. My skirt must have ridden up at some point, and he was teasing. I'm so damned embarrassed. I apologized, but now that you've told me all this, I'm going to be mortified facing him on Monday morning."

Sophie's laughter drifted across the phone lines. "Maybe it's just the step you two need to take your relationship to the next level."

"I don't know what you're talking about."

"Oh for heaven's sake, you two have been moving around each other like chess pieces for months. I've seen the way he looks at you when you're not looking. And if last night's any sort of indicator, you've got your knickers in a twist over him."

"I … you …"

"Uh … uh … cat got your tongue? Or is my assessment closer to home than you realize?"

"After Omar … well you know …"

"Gary isn't just any man. He's your swan."

"I beg your pardon?"

"Poppy can explain it better. They mate for life. Ian and I think, and even Poppy thinks, Gary is your swan. You're just having such a hard time getting past your trauma with Omar that you can't see it. But, I'm not worried. Gary seems to be the patient type. I suspect he'll wait until you come around."

"Come around?"

"Yes. Come around. Listen, I've got to bolt. We'll talk later. Bye."

The line went dead and I stared at the phone. My thoughts churned with the revelations Sophie had just dumped on my head.

Was I ready to move on to another relationship, and if so, could it be Gary?

It could, of course, be Gary. I trusted him implicitly, and if I were honest with myself, sexual feelings for him had been bubbling to the surface. He was the cute boy next door with a spattering of freckles across his nose, sandy-brown hair cropped close, and—let's face it – he kept in shape. The arms and chest that comforted me last night were solid. Even the intense stares he'd given me at times had butterflies flapping in my belly. On the other hand, there were similarities between Gary's job and Omar's that gave me pause, like the fact that he carried a gun.

Still ... was Sophie right? Was Gary waiting for me to come around or indicate that I was willing to deepen our relationship?

Chapter Six

I didn't have to worry about an embarrassing moment on Monday morning, because Gary didn't bring Annie up to the house. He kissed her good-bye at the car and waved to me as I stood in the doorway.

Sanvi arrived on time, and I pulled into Le Pinceau's parking lot at twenty to ten. Kaitlin drove up just as I stepped from the car, and I waited for her to join me.

"The courier is coming today to get the Camponetti for Leighton. I'll need you to man the phones while I help them crate it for delivery."

"No problem, boss. Anything else on the agenda today?"

"Karl will be in this afternoon to work on cleaning the …"

"Watch out!" Kaitlin grabbed my arm and pulled me back from the front door. "What the hell is that?" She hid behind me and looked over my shoulder.

A bloody, twisted rat lay in front of the door. It must have been fresh, because it wasn't covered in ants, nor did it look as though the vultures had dined on it yet. I had a tabby in college who presented me with the occasional trophy mouse or bird. This disgusting specimen looked similar. *Charming.*

"It's a rat. Looks like a cat left us a present."

"That's disgusting. I'm not touching it."

I didn't want to touch it either. But I couldn't leave it sitting in front of the entryway of the gallery for customers to see. I stepped over the mangled mess. "Come on. There are some gloves in the back and a dustpan."

"Uh, uh. I never signed up for rat disposal." Kaitlin backed away shaking her head.

I sighed at her immaturity. "Neither did I, but it's got to be moved. You can either scoop it up in the dustpan or hold the trash bag."

"No scooping. I'll hold the bag."

"Very well."

Five minutes later, both of us wore white rubber gloves and Kaitlin stood bent over with her arms stretched out as far as they could go, holding the bag toward me. Wielding the red plastic dustpan, I crouched and quickly shoved it at the rat. Unfortunately, instead of rolling onto the pan, it rolled away from it.

"Eeep!" Kaitlin dropped the bag and danced away. "It's *alive.*"

Oh for heaven's sake. "It's not alive. I need a stick or something to help shove it onto the pan."

"Whatever. I'm resigning from the rat disposal team."

I grimaced. "Fine. Go get me a stick about yay thick and two feet long." My hands splayed out to demonstrate.

Kaitlin headed over to the small treed area next to the parking lot, and I squatted down to make another attempt to scoop up the carcass. No luck.

It was this ignoble position in which Gary found me. Luckily, I'd worn slacks today instead of a dress, so there was no chance of flashing him my stockings. His unmarked cruiser rolled up to the curb and the window slid down. My face burned.

"What are you doing?"

"Trying to dispose of a dead rat." I shoved at it again.

The car shifted into park and he stepped out. "Where did that come from?"

"I suspect a wandering tomcat left it behind." I continued to regard the rat, too embarrassed to look at him.

"Hmph."

"Here, boss, will this do?" Kaitlin trotted down the sidewalk brandishing a good-sized stick.

"That's fine. Thanks."

Kaitlin gave Gary the once over and pasted on a winning smile. "So, who's this?"

"This is Detective Sumner, my neighbor. Kaitlin Froggett, gallery assistant."

He nodded, and I took the stick from her. "Gary, could you hold the trash bag?"

"No problem."

He lifted up the bag and held it open. I pushed the rat onto the plastic pan with the stick, scooped it up, and dropped everything into the bag.

"Don't you want the pan?"

"Nope."

He tightened the bag.

"I'll take that." Gary passed it into my waiting hand. "Kaitlin, fill up a bucket of water from the back room and wash down the sidewalk, please."

Kaitlin frowned but headed into the gallery.

To my mortification, Gary followed me around the side of the building to the dumpster. "So what brings you to this neck of the woods?"

"I heard from Claire. Or actually, her lawyer."

All thoughts of the weekend's embarrassment disappeared. "Oh, dear. I thought we hadn't seen the end of it. What does she want?" I stripped off the gloves and tossed them in after the bag.

"Partial custody."

"Partial custody?" I finally faced him and noticed the tension in his face. "How is she going to manage that? Doesn't she live in Europe now?"

"It's unclear where she's living now. She listed a local marina as her current address."

"What does your lawyer say? Can she get it?"

"Doubtful, but she can waste my time and money fighting for it."

"So what are we going to do?"

"*We* aren't doing anything. This is my fight. I have a meeting with the lawyer tomorrow, and a hearing has been scheduled in January. I just figured I should let you know what's going on."

"Hey, now." I crossed my arms and frowned. "Annie's a part of my family, too. This isn't a time to go all macho 'I can do this myself.'" I used finger quotes. "It's time to circle the wagons. At minimum, I can be a witness for you. Provide testimony."

His brows crunched and those amber eyes surveyed me. An inappropriate rush of heat bloomed in my cheeks and I swear my nipples hardened. *What the hell?* I pivoted on my kitten heel and marched back toward the front. "C'mon inside. I'll pour you a cup of coffee and we'll take a few minutes to strategize."

• • •

A vision of her splayed across the bed—skirt riding up—flashed through his mind as he watched her cute backside click-click away in those little heels. He shook himself free of the memory when she turned the corner. *I've got to stop letting this woman get inside my head.*

After parking his cruiser next to her sedan, he rejoined Holly in her office.

"Chocolate hazelnut, fresh out of the pot." She closed the door behind him and pointed to a mug of steaming coffee on her desk; two packets of sugar and a plastic stirrer lay next to it.

"Thanks."

"So what are we going to do about Claire until the hearing? Can she see Annie in the meantime?"

"My lawyer says no." He poured the sugar into the mug. "He said it will look bad at the hearing if she tries something like what she did last week. She's been warned by the lawyers on both sides.

I just hope she's in an appropriate mental state to understand and comply."

"Mmm." Holly sipped her coffee. "Where is she getting the money for this? I don't see Thor the boyfriend as the type to be interested in having someone else's kid tagging along. First of all, Annie wouldn't fit in his Porsche."

"Thor," he snorted. "Good one. Perfect description."

Her lids drooped and she gave that smirk he loved. It was just a small twist of her lips. He returned his gaze to the coffee mug in his hand and focused on the gallery's red logo. "I'm not sure where the money's coming from. Claire's cunning enough to have acquired herself a benefactor. But who knows? Maybe she sold a piece of jewelry someone gave her."

"We'd better talk to Sanvi about the circumstances. She handled last week's situation well, but it would be best if she were on guard. I could see Claire trying to surprise them or 'accidentally' run into them at a store or something."

"You're right. I'll call her."

Business concluded, an awkward silence reigned. He cleared his throat, Holly opened her mouth, and they spoke at the same time.

"Listen, about the …" she said.

"I should …"

They both stopped and Holly's cheeks turned a lovely pink.

"I'm sorry," he said. "You were about to say?"

"I, uh, wanted to apologize again for the other night. Sophie told me that I pretty much made a fool of myself. And if I said or did anything inappropriate toward you, I'm very sorry." The last bit came out in a rush.

"No, I'm sorry about the stocking crack."

She cleared her throat and looked away from him. "Did I, uh, flash you?"

"Only accidentally." He shifted uncomfortably. "After you'd passed out. It was ungentlemanly of me to say anything." Her neck was flushed deep red, and he felt bad to have embarrassed her with his flirtation.

"I don't …" A knock at the door interrupted whatever she was about to say.

Kaitlin stuck her head in. "Boss, the courier is here for the Camponetti."

"I'll be right there. I'm sorry, Gary; I need to take care of this."

He rose. "No problem. I'd better get going anyway. When should I expect to see you tonight?"

"Around six thirty. Please let me know if you hear anything more from Claire." She came around the desk and ushered him out.

"Will do," he tossed over his shoulder.

His phone rang on the way to the car. It was the supervising detective; they'd caught a new case. He punched the address into his GPS and motored away. Holly's citrus scent lingered, and he mentally kicked himself for teasing her about the stockings. He should have known she wouldn't appreciate it. Even with the Claire business and work weighing on his mind, Holly always seemed to play around the edges. And he really didn't know what to do about it.

Chapter Seven

The courier's van rolled away with the Camponetti painting wrapped and crated well enough to withstand a drop from a four-story building. The gallery owners, Bianca and Marcello, were returning to town today from their biannual trip to Italy; there were a few things I needed to straighten up and a weekly report to prepare before they arrived. However, as it had been doing all morning, my mind had trouble focusing on work. Even though Gary and I apologized and moved on, the fact that I behaved so inappropriately continued to weigh heavily. And Claire's efforts to inveigle herself back into Annie's life frustrated and angered me, too. I didn't want his ex in our lives, and if she gained any sort of custody, "in our lives," was exactly where she'd be. It was difficult to let it go; my head was a hot mess.

I returned to my office to find my sister in the green-striped guest chair, her sneakers resting on my glass desk.

"Hey!" I smacked at a foot. "Did Mom raise you in a barn?"

Her feet hit the floor and she grinned, unabashed.

"What are you doing here?"

"Since you sold the last one, I've brought you another Hartland original." She snorted and jerked her head to the left.

Propped against the wall stood a 20- by 30-inch modern painting of bold reds and yellows with a wave of blue through the middle; it reminded me of a fiery sunset. Last year, when I spent a time at Ian's, I admired a painting that Sophie created for one of her clients. It captured a feeling of movement that other amateurs never seemed to achieve. When I took the job at Le Pinceau, I asked her to paint me something to display at the gallery. Soph laughed, disbelieving that her "bathroom art" would be fancy enough, but after weeks of my entreating, she finally caved and passed along something she'd planned to trash because the colors didn't quite fit the color scheme of a client's remodel. The gallery owners purchased her first piece. Once Sophie's engagement to Ian hit the papers, she became a minor celebrity—to her chagrin—and her paintings rarely stayed on the gallery wall longer than two or three weeks.

I picked it up and held it at arm's length. "I love it. It's something I could wake up to every morning."

"Take it. I'll paint something else." She slouched back in the chair.

"Oh, no. As a matter of fact, I might have a potential buyer."

"Then sell it and take the commission. I'll paint you something else." It blew my mind that her art came so easily. I envied her the ease of creation.

"About that—we aren't doing another fifty-fifty. I'm reducing my commission."

"I've done the research, Holly. I know that fifty-fifty is a standard for galleries."

"Yes, but I hardly have to lift a finger to sell your stuff. It's not like I put on a show for you. I actually have a half dozen clients who asked me to call them whenever you bring something in."

"So? It's easy money. Just take the fifty percent and shut up."

"I'm not a charity case. I'm doing well with this job, you know," I snapped. Sophie had taken to giving me handouts ever since I'd arrived, a bedraggled mess, on her back porch. She set up a college fund for Eva with half of the money she made off the paintings, and I found it belittling that my sister didn't think I was successful enough to support myself and my daughter.

"Enough, Holly!" She shot out of her chair, her brows furrowed, and an angry frown marred her pretty features. "I'm tired of this misconstrued idea you have that I think you're a charity case. I'll admit, when you first moved here, I helped you out financially. But now, your rent pays the full mortgage on the house, and, per your request, I've stopped buying clothes for Eva except for holidays and birthdays."

"Ian snuck her a Lakers jersey last week." I crossed my arms.

"Cripes." She threw up her hands. "That's Ian. He loves the Lakers and would give a jersey to every kid from here to Kentucky if he could. He's given me three. You don't want him to give gifts to Eva? Then you talk to him." She poked me in the shoulder. "I'm tired of this. I know you're a highly qualified curator making a good salary. You're successful. I get it. What you don't seem to get is that you're my sister. I'm thrilled you moved here with Eva and I get to see you all the time. I'm in a position to buy you and my niece nice things. I like doing it, and not because I think you're a charity case. Stop being such a whiny bitch, and just say thank you."

"As for the commission, it's fifty friggin' fifty or I'll take my damn bathroom art elsewhere! This isn't a handout, Holly. It's business. Act like it." Sophie's finger waved in my face, and I felt like a chastised five-year-old.

"I'm sorry. You're right," I mumbled.

She harrumphed and returned to the chair. "What is going on with you anyway? You've been acting weird for the past week. Longer than the incident at the party. Omar's not getting out of jail early, is he? Is there something wrong with Eva? I feel like you're hiding something from me."

My sister knew me too well. "I didn't tell you, because it feels as though I'm always dumping my problems on you, but Gary's ex-wife, Claire, showed up last week."

"The psycho who left in the middle of the night?"

"The very one. And Gary told me just today that she's looking to gain partial custody."

"I don't imagine he's too thrilled about that."

"No, he's not."

"What about you? How does that make you feel?"

"Geez. You sound like my shrink."

She grinned. "And?"

"And, I'm pissed. Claire's a flighty fruitcake who ran out on her husband and young child. I'm pissed she wants to push her way back in. Gary doesn't deserve to have to deal with more of her shit."

"Don't hold back, sis. Tell me what you really think," Sophie snorted.

"I think she's a nutball." I explained the incident and her Porsche-driving, blond superhero.

"You know what I think?" she asked with a smirk and raised brow.

"What do you think?" I crossed my arms.

"You're jealous."

"What?"

"You're jealous. You don't want her back in Annie's life, but you also don't want her in Gary's either."

"What the hell are you talking about? I don't want her anywhere near my kid. And if she's around Annie, she'll be around Eva."

"And … you don't want her around Gary either. Admit it."

"Okay, fine, yes, I don't want her bothering Gary either." I threw up my hands. "He's got a stressful job, and he's put up with enough of her crap. And the way she was falling all over Gary. 'Let's get some coffee,'" I mimicked. "Ugh. What a phony."

"Omigod. You're like a mighty lioness pacing in front of her mate, growling at the rest of the pride. Staking your claim."

I halted my pacing.

"She worries you. You're afraid he's still drawn to her, and that makes you jealous."

I sucked wind and opened my mouth to lambast Sophie. But nothing came out.

"Let me ask you this. What if it wasn't Claire? Gary's a good-looking guy with a steady job. How would you feel if he started dating someone from the precinct? Or the barista at Starbucks? Have you two even talked about dating other people?"

Dating? Gary? The idea made me physically shudder.

Oh ... my ... God. Sophie is right. We'd worked our way into a companionable relationship, similar to married couples, only without the sex. The thought of a third party changing that disturbed me. My feelings for Gary ran much deeper than I'd realized, and if I were honest, my body had been sexually turned on by him for some time.

Sophie's phone chirped, interrupting my train of thought. "Crap. It's my assistant; I'm supposed to meet her at a potential client's house in half an hour. I completely spaced it out." She looked down at her jeans with a hole in the knee. "Crap, I'm not dressed appropriately, and I don't have time to go back to the house."

"Here." I took off my red blazer and held it out. "Put this on and trade shoes with me."

Even though Sophie had curves to envy, she'd be able to wear the jacket unbuttoned. She slipped it on, toed off her sneakers and slid her feet into my kitten heels, tucked in her girl-cut, navy T-shirt, and rolled down the jeans. The transformation went from weekend casual to designer chic.

"Take my earrings, too." I unhooked the sterling silver hoops. "Now you look like a design consultant with that breezy, creative touch."

"You're a doll. Listen, I'm sorry about Claire. We'll talk more later. Just think about what I said and how you behaved toward Gary when your inhibitions were down."

She exited with a wave, leaving my mind in more of a muddle than it was this morning.

My thoughts still spiraled the next morning on the drive to work when my phone rang.

"Hey, it's Kaitlin. There's another rat at the front door. I'm not touching it."

"Another one? Seriously?"

"Yeah. The trap you set last night worked. He's squished in half. It's pretty gruesome."

"What trap? I didn't set a trap."

"Well, someone did. 'Cause it caught a big, fat one."

Five minutes later, I motored into the parking lot and hopped out. Kaitlin leaned against the front window, arms crossed, about fifteen feet from the front door. Sure enough, a juicy rat was caught in a trap right in front of the door … again.

"Who the hell set this trap?"

"Dunno. But, I'm not touching it." Kaitlin shuddered and pulled a face.

Bianca or Marcello must have come by the studio after closing.

"So you said. Go find another stick, please." I keyed in and stepped over the rat. Since the dustpan hadn't been replaced, I searched the backroom for something to scoop the rat up. I finally grabbed a small plastic wastebasket with a bag inside. I tilted it on the side and, with the stick Kaitlin found, I shoved the trap, rat and all, into the bin. I knotted the sack, took it 'round to the dumpster, and mentally added "contact exterminator" on my to-do list for the day.

Chapter Eight

The passenger door popped open and the confidential informant slid into the seat. His eyes darted warily around the moderately busy strip mall parking lot, and he tugged his sweatshirt's hoodie farther forward.

"Did you make sure you weren't followed?"

"I took two busses. I didn't see nobody."

That didn't necessarily mean anything.

"You should be fine."

"So what can I do for LA's finest today?" Raoul nervously tapped a tattooed hand on his knee.

Raoul was a gangbanger Gary had acquired back during his days as a homicide detective. He'd had a third offense drug rap and was looking at some serious time in the clink. Gary was able to arrange a deal in order to get him to roll on a shooter. After Gary moved into the financial crimes unit he didn't have much use for Raoul, but every so often the gang unit or homicide needed someone on the inside, and Raoul was always happy to pocket the department's snitch money.

"Word on the street is there's a new banger in town looking to make his mark and take over some of the Black P-Stones' territory. Bodies are starting to turn up. You know anything about that?" Gary asked.

"That depends ... what is it worth?" Raoul slouched lower in the seat.

"The usual."

"I don't think I know anything then."

Gary's phone vibrated with a new text. "Think you might know something for an extra fifty?"

"I don't know, man. There's a lot of information bouncing around up in *mi cabeza.*" He tapped his head. "Ju know?"

The text came from Holly.

My car got broken into at the gallery. Police are on the way. I think I know who did it.

Who?

Gary turned to Raoul after hitting send on his text. "Think about it. Maybe something will come to you."

"I might remember for an extra hundred."

Cokehead from party.

Gary's pulse accelerated to DEFCON 2 and he barked "Get out." at Raoul.

"Hey, man, I thought this was a negotiation."

"Negotiation over." Gary started the car. "Either tell me now and get your extra fifty or get out."

"Okay, okay, man. Relax." He jammed his hands into his sweatshirt pockets. "Ju are looking for a skinny black dude, goes by the name Diamond Back, or D-Back. Rumor has he come from the Oakdale gang up in Frisco."

"Is he the trigger man?"

Raoul shrugged.

Gary squinted at him.

"Seriously, *gringo*. That's all I know." Raoul held out a dirty hand and Gary slapped the cash in it.

"Give me a call if you think of anything else. It might be worth something," he said as Raoul opened the car door.

"Hey, next time can we meet in a parking lot with some titty bars or something? There's nothing to do out here with these Starbucks-drinking, suburban mamas."

"Shut the door." It slammed closed and Gary peeled out.

Twenty minutes later, he wheeled into the gallery parking lot. Holly and the assistant, Kailey or Katie or something, stood next to her. Both posed with stiff, crossed arms, as a uniformed officer spoke to them. Holly's tight features softened slightly as he approached.

"I didn't think you were coming," she said.

"I was in the middle of something and had to finish up."

"Who are you?" the officer asked.

"Officer Mahoney, this is Detective Sumner," Holly introduced the two.

"Who called in the detective squad for a smash and grab?" Mahoney frowned and stuck out his chest.

"No one called it in. I'm Ms. Hartland's neighbor, so she texted me. What happened?"

"See for yourself." She tilted her chin toward the silver Kia.

He walked around to the passenger side to find the window broken and a mangled rat lying on the front seat. Removing his sunglasses, he scrutinized the destruction. He didn't like it. The drug addict's final words as Ziggy dragged him out of the party, rang in his ears. *Damn! I should have gotten more information on that jackass. I knew he was bad news.* This cowardly act of vandalism and intimidation seemed par for the course from an asshole flying higher than Delta. The officer joined him beside the vehicle.

"Looks like he used that brick." He pointed at the object on the floor in front of the seat. "Then threw the rat in afterward."

Thank you, Captain Obvious. Gary straightened and regarded Holly over the car's roof. "When did it happen?"

She shrugged. "Kaitlin was gone from eleven until about three, and I was in back most of that time, working with one of the art restorers. He left out the back door about two thirty."

"What about your security cameras?" He glanced up at the globe under the eaves of the overhang.

Holly shook her head. "It faces the door; not pointed at the parking lot."

"Did you notice when you returned, Kaitlin?" Gary's eyes shifted to the young assistant taking a drag from an unsteady cigarette.

"No." Her lips pursed and she blew out the smoke. "It was fine when I left. This afternoon I drove around back to drop off supplies. My car is still back there."

"I went out to get something from my car about three thirty. That's when I found it," Holly explained.

Unless there was a witness, it would be hard to pin anything on the suspect. "Canvass the neighborhood, see if there are any witnesses," he instructed Officer Mahoney. "Check security cameras in the area—maybe they caught something. Also, see if you can get fingerprints off the brick."

Mahoney eyeballed him. "You're asking for a lot of resources for a broken window," he said in low tones.

"It's intimidation and retribution. This is the second rat Ms. Hartland has been presented with."

"Third."

Both the men looked up. Gary didn't realize Holly had approached the vehicle. "Third? When?"

"Two days ago. Another rat was in front of the door."

"She's right. Squished in a trap. It was gross," Kaitlin piped in.

"If it was in front of the door, you should have him on the video surveillance."

Holly flushed. "The system needs upgrading. We only have space to retain the videos for two weeks. I … wasn't thinking … didn't make a connection. The files were deleted yesterday."

"Did you keep the trap?" Gary asked.

Holly shook her head. "I thought one of the gallery owners put it down."

Double damn! How did I not get this guy's name? "Have you called your sister yet?"

"No. But I'm not sure she knows who he was. Ian would probably know."

He pulled out his cell phone and dialed Ian O'Connor.

"What can I do for you, detective?" Ian answered.

"Remember the drug addict from your party that you and Ziggy threw out?"

"Of course. Why?"

"We think he's trying to intimidate Holly. Someone's been leaving her dead rats. Today they broke the window on her car and threw a rat in the front seat."

"Bollocks."

"Do you have a name?"

"Let me ring a few people. I'll get back to you." The line went dead.

"Why do we think it's this guy?" the officer asked.

Holly rolled her eyes and huffed "I *ratted* him out."

"She found him snorting lines in the bathroom," Gary explained.

Realization dawned across Mahoney's face.

Gary's phone rang. "Detective Sumner."

"The fuck nugget you're looking for is Trey Holtzman."

"Thanks, Ian."

"Sumner, you got this one?"

"I'm on it." He hung up. "Trey Holtzman."

The officer returned to his cruiser, and Gary's phone rang again. "Sumner."

"Hey man, long time no see. I might have some more information for ju on that ... person we talked about. Ju know ... earlier."

Gary eyed Holly and Kaitlin; the latter stubbed out her cigarette, and the two fell into stilted conversation. "Not now. I'll call you back later."

"Okay, man. But I might not remember later."

Damn it, Raoul, you better not be wasting my time. Gary turned and meandered far enough away from the car that he wouldn't be overheard. "What is it?"

"Depends. How much is it worth to ju?"

"Since I don't know what you think you're giving me, it's worth nothing at the moment."

"What if I could tell ju where the dude was planning to hang out tonight?"

Shit. If Raoul wasn't yanking his chain, the information would definitely be worth something to the homicide department. "Two hundred for time and place."

"Two fifty."

"When and where?"

"Thirty minutes, under the 5th Street Bridge."

He'd never be able to make it in half an hour. "Forty-five."

"Fine. Don't be late, man. I don't like hangin' around so close to home. Ju know what I mean?"

"I'll be there." Holly's elbow rested on Officer Mahoney's open door, and the two of them were speaking in low tones. "What did you find?"

"Well, Ms. Hartland identified Trey Holtzman as the man from the party. He's got a DUI and has been arrested twice, but the charges were dropped."

"What were the charges for?"

"Drug possession."

"Sounds like our man. They should have his fingerprints on file."

"We'll get the brick checked and dust the car, too."

Gary gave a sharp nod and pulled Holly aside. He ran a frustrated hand through his hair. "Listen, I'm sorry, but I'm working another case and I've got to go. Can you get a ride home with Kaitlin?" It tore him apart to leave her—her eyes were too wide and filled with vulnerability—but Raoul hadn't given him much of a choice. He had to stick with department priorities. Even though this wasn't his case, he knew how important the information could be for the boys in homicide. Taking D-Back off the streets could stop an impending gang war and would likely reduce the future body count.

"My sister texted while you were on the phone. She's on her way."

"Good. I'll catch up with you tonight." He kissed her forehead. "Don't worry. We'll find this guy. It won't happen again."

Chapter Nine

Sophie and I sat in the kitchen watching Annie and Eva in the backyard, giggling and whooping as Sanvi chased them around, with the intrepid Sirius running and barking at their antics.

"Are you sure you don't want me to stay the night?" Sophie asked for the third time.

"I told you, I'm fine." I'm not certain whom I was trying to reassure with that statement–Sophie or myself. The initial adrenaline of fear had ebbed, leaving behind a jittery stomach and unaccountable fatigue. However, I felt safe enough at home with my alarm, and I honestly had no interest in having my sister hover over me like a wolf guarding its cub.

"What about Ziggy? You want me to send him over?"

I shuddered and rolled my eyes at the idea of having Ziggy prowling around my house. Don't get me wrong, I had a special affection for Ziggy, but no real interest in hiring his services for a couple of rats and a broken window.

"Perish the thought."

"Do you need me to pick you up tomorrow to get the car?"

"No, I'll call a cab or something."

"Are you sure? What about getting your car fixed?"

"I'll be fine. Your client is halfway across town, nowhere near me. I'll figure something out. Bianca told me to take the rest of the week off. The insurance company will cover the damage, and they gave me the name of a shop that can take care of replacing the window. I'll get a rental while it's being fixed, so … really, it's all taken care of. Because of Gary, the police are taking this seriously. I'm sure they'll find Trey Holtzman soon." I sipped the wine in an effort to calm my nerves. Eva and Annie had reversed the attack and caught Sanvi, and the three of them lay on the ground, laughing as the girls tickled the nanny. Sirius circled the pile, pink tongue lolling to the side.

The doorbell rang and Sophie jumped up. "I'll get that for you."

She returned to the kitchen following Gary. I rose and placed my hands in his. Perhaps it was a more intimate gesture than normal, but at this moment it seemed the most natural thing in the world, not unlike his kiss to my forehead back at the gallery. An instant hum of energy flowed from the heat of his hands up my arms, acting as a balm to the tension running through my body.

"Good news," he said without a hint of a smile. "Trey Holtzman's car was observed speeding through the parking lot, and it was caught on a traffic camera running a red light less than a block away. It's enough to bring him in for questioning."

I squeezed his rough hands in relief. "What about fingerprints?"

"Not sure yet. Mahoney said they lifted a partial, but the results aren't back yet to see if they're a match."

"Thank you." I scrutinized the dark depths of his gaze and allowed his presence to calm me in a way that my sister's company never could. We stared an unaccountable amount of time until Sophie cleared her throat.

"Well, it looks like you have everything in hand. So I think I'll get the girls and go."

Jerked from the spell, Gary released me and gazed over his shoulder. "Thanks for staying with her. What are you doing with the girls?"

"No problem." She winked, then pulled open the back door and whistled. "*Sirius,* come on, boy. Dinnertime, girls. Aunt Sophie is taking you two out for pizza."

Sirius scrambled through the door with tail wagging, closely followed by the children. Chaos ensued for the next ten minutes as we removed their dusty sneakers and replaced them with nicer shoes, ran a brush through tangled curls, gathered coats, washed hands, and wiped dirty faces with a wet cloth. The cacophony exited with Sophie as she left with a hyper Lab and two excited little girls yammering at top volume about their favorite Disney princesses.

"See you in an hour." The door closed with a thump, and I rejoined Sanvi and Gary in the kitchen.

"So, like I said, I haven't seen anything," Sanvi said.

"Are we talking about Claire?" I asked.

Gary nodded. "I was just getting an update. Making sure Sanvi hadn't seen or heard anything untoward. So far, so good."

"Can't you put one of your fancy police trackers or something on her so you know where she is all the time, like embed a microchip under her skin while she sleeps? They did that to a terrorist on *LA Heat* recently," Sanvi pointed out.

"I'm not sure that would be an option, but couldn't we track her phone?" I asked, warming to Sanvi's idea.

Gary rolled his eyes and grimaced at our bright ideas. "Well, ladies, as lovely an idea as that would be, there are all these pesky laws about invasion of privacy, warrants, probable cause, and such. So, unfortunately there's nothing I can do at the moment. Second, remind me to have Ian introduce me to some of *LA Heat*'s screenwriters sometime so I can set them straight."

Sanvi shrugged and gathered her phone and purse. "If you don't need anything else, I'll be heading out then." Gary shouldered her overflowing tote, a necessary nanny accessory, and escorted her out. Meanwhile, I stared sightlessly out the back door. The dead rat, broken glass, Trey's threat at Sophie's party, Kaitlin's hand wavering as she smoked her cigarette ... the thoughts tumbled 'round and 'round.

"Here's your mail." He startled me, dropping the pile on the table. I checked my watch and realized that Gary had been gone about twenty minutes.

"Everything okay with Sanvi?" I pick up the mail and didn't hear Gary's response. Sitting atop the pile was the familiar bold scrawl of Omar's father. *Great, just when I thought this day couldn't get any worse.* I'd stopped reading the missives months ago, dropping them unopened in a shoebox on the top shelf of my closet. I saved them in case my ex-in-laws ever took me back to court. The shaking returned, and I picked up the pile in an effort to hide it, shuffling through the missives, pretending to read them, to cover up the real purpose of burying the letter at the bottom of the pack.

"Holly. Stop. Forget the mail." Gary pulled the pile out of my hands and reclaimed them. "Talk to me."

He likely assumed my reaction had to do with the vandalism to my car. It did and it didn't. "It's nothing. I'm fine."

"Your hands are freezing. You're pale and shaking. It isn't nothing."

"I just wonder how I keep ending up in these situations."

"I've wondered that myself." He drew me into his arms, and I laid my cheek against his chest.

His hand rubbed up and down my back in a soothing manner, and he made shushing noises. Eventually, his body heat seeped into me and the shivers receded. I drew in a breath; he smelled of soap and spicy aftershave and … that musk that can only be described as man. Surreptitiously, I inhaled his scent, which started a different kind of quiver in my stomach. My arms moved from Gary's shoulders up to his neck, and I allowed my fingers to play with the short, clipped hair at the base. His arms tightened, his nose brushed against my tresses, and his hands paused their rubbing.

I shifted my head back. Our mouths were a hairsbreadth apart, and Gary gazed at me with blazing eyes, turning my belly quiver into liquid heat that began spreading through my limbs. I waited for his mouth to descend upon mine, but he held off, and I realized he waited for me to make the first move.

Of their own volition, my heels lifted from the ground to close the gap. Our lips met, supple warmth softly testing the waters. Gary drew his tongue across my lower lip and I allowed him access. The liquid heat exploded into a raging inferno as our tongues danced. Gary's arms tightened and I pressed myself into him, plastering myself against his hardened chest.

I sucked on his bottom lip. Stroking turned to kneading as his hands massaged my backside, pulling me closer. I felt his erection against my pelvic bone and tilted my head back with a moan. His lips descended lower, feeding on the sensitive part of my neck as my fingers played with the short hairs of his buzz cut. My senses tingled with electric fire, aware of each touch and caress.

The doorbell rang and then the door popped opened. "It's just me. I forgot my phone." Sanvi's voiced echoed down the hall.

Gary and I jumped apart like teenagers caught making out in the back of the car.

"Found it, see you tomorrow," she called and the door shut.

A hand flew to my kiss-swollen lips; my body tingled where it had been plastered against his. His chest heaved up and down as he struggled to calm his breathing.

"That was … uh …"

Eyes darkened with desire scorched me, and before I could think or say something foolish, I threw myself back into his arms, carrying on where we left off. Hands rubbed and stroked as tongues licked and tasted. Gary unbuttoned my blouse and his fingers slipped in, massaging my breast through the satin bra, turning my nipples into hard peaks. I think I whimpered.

"Holly."

I moaned and nibbled a path along his chin.

"Holly … honey, hold up."

"No," I whispered. "We don't have to stop."

"Sweetheart." He gently pushed me back. "It's my phone."

I finally registered the jarring ring.

"I'm in the middle of a case. I have to take it."

I nodded, pulled my blouse closed, and stepped back.

"Detective Sumner," Gary answered.

I hot-footed it to my room to gain distance … and sanity. Once the door closed, I leaned against it with eyes shut tight. *Holy cow, that was hot and sexy … and … oh my. Who knew Gary had so much hunger hiding behind his unflappable cop façade?*

My hormones continued to rage, leaving behind needy aches throughout my body. In an effort to calm them, I kicked off my shoes and shed my work clothes for jeans and a comfy sweatshirt. In the bathroom, I did a breath check and decided to brush my teeth. Afterward, I ran a comb through my tousled hair and paused. The kiss had been a hundred times better than I'd ever imagined it could be. My cheeks glowed pink and my eyes were dark with remnants of our passion. For a moment, I closed my eyes and relived our moment of ardent recklessness.

"Holly?" A knock sounded on my bedroom door.

"Just a sec." I finished with my hair, rubbed away the mascara flakes from under my eyes, and swiped on some lip gloss. When I opened the door, Gary stood leaning against the jam, closer than I expected.

"That was officer Mahoney. Looks like the partial was a match. They sent a squad car over to Holtzman's house, but he wasn't there. They've put out a BOLO."

"BOLO?"

"Be on the look out."

"Okay. What do I need to do?"

"For the moment, nothing. When they find him, he'll be put in a lineup to see if the witness can identify him as the man speeding through the parking lot."

"Thanks for letting me know."

"We need to talk about what just happened."

I remained mute, waiting for him to take the lead.

"Look." He rubbed a hand through his hair. For once his ever calm, composed cop demeanor was flustered, and he seemed to struggle with what to say.

"That was interesting."

"Holly, I … hell."

"Regrets?" I fiddled with an earring.

His eyes narrowed. "No. You?"

My ego sat up and I gave him a sly smile. "Me neither."

He released a windy breath, then sent me a toe-curling grin. "What do you think we should do about it?"

I closed the gap and pressed myself against him. He didn't need further invitation. In nanoseconds his lips were back to plundering mine as we picked up where we'd left off. Warm fingers combed through my hair. He walked me backward until the backs of my knees hit the bed and I lay down, pulling him with me. As I cupped his jaw, our lips came together and I tasted his essence, enjoying the touch and intimacy of the simple kiss. He nipped around the edges of my lips, worked his way across my closed lids, and, brushing aside my hair, his lips worked their way to the sensitive shell of my ear.

I sighed with pleasure when Gary suddenly jerked upright. Excited chattering and the bark of a large, black Lab burst through the front door.

Jesus, the stars are not aligning for us.

"We're back," Annie called.

"Damn it," he mumbled.

"Argh! Didn't they just leave?" I rested my head against his heaving chest for a moment before separating.

"About an hour ago." He kissed my forehead and moved off down the hall. "How was dinner?" I heard him ask the girls.

Sure enough, the clock showed it was just over an hour since Sophie left with the girls. *I guess time flies when you're having fun.*

I heaved myself off the bed and joined the troops. Annie chattered away at Gary while Eva ran in a circle around the kitchen island, followed by a red balloon attached to her wrist.

Sophie was holding Sirius's collar to keep him from chasing Eva. She took in my appearance as I entered the kitchen—her eyes flared and flashed to Gary before returning back to me. Surreptitiously, I finger combed my rumpled hair. The right side of her mouth quirked up and was matched with a raised eyebrow.

Eva launched herself at my legs. "Mommy, look. B-loon. I got a red one."

I crouched and picked her up. "I see that. Did you have fun with Aunt Sophie?"

She nodded, then produced a big yawn.

"Did they behave themselves?" Gary asked.

"Who, the girls?" Sophie grinned slyly at us. "Oh, yes, *they* behaved."

"Great. Thanks so much for taking them. We shouldn't keep you. I'm sure Ian will be wondering where you are."

She rolled her eyes at my redirection. "Very well. It looks like Gary has things under control here. C'mon, Sirius. Time to go. I'll give you a call to check up on you tomorrow." She winked and headed out.

"Daddy, I'm tired," Annie said.

Gary looked over his shoulder at Eva and me. He pointed to his chest and mouthed the words—*stay the night?*

In the past, Gary had been welcome to spend the night. However, our small indiscretion had just changed the balance of power. Since it seemed the police were on to Trey, my fears about him receded. I needed a night alone to wrap my head around my interlude with Gary and to decide what to do about it.

"I'll be fine. Bring Annie over if you get called in."

He didn't argue, and I figured he might need time to think as well.

• • •

"And they lived happily ever after." Gary closed the book. Annie's eyelashes brushed her cheeks, and her breath was slow and even. He pulled up the covers, turned out the lights, and left the door cracked. Once in the kitchen, he stood staring in the fridge. *Damn, I wish I weren't on call. I could really use that beer.* Finally, the sexy dreams he'd had about Holly had come to fruition, and then they were hastily shut down. It left the two of them in a strange limbo, and left him unsure as to how to approach her the next time they met.

The fridge door slammed shut and he threw himself down on the couch, flipping aimlessly through channels, searching for some program to take his mind off the visions of Holly— her swollen lips; open shirt; sexy, rumpled hair; desire–filled dark eyes as she crooked a come-hither finger at him.

He rubbed his own eyes with the heels of his hands and groaned. Generally a patient man, he was finding his patience waning and his baser instincts trying to take over where she was concerned. He stopped the channel surfing on a 24-hour news network and made an effort to dismiss all thoughts of Holly and tune in to the latest update on foreign affairs.

He achieved little success in his endeavor.

Chapter Ten

The door opened to reveal my sister's best friend, elegantly dressed in an emerald-green pants suit.

"Good morning. Sophie told me all about your vehicular problems, and she thought you might need a lift to your car this morning." I gaped at Poppy as she swept past me in a cloud of Chanel No. 5, strutting toward the back of the house. "But first, where are those adorable girls? Eva? Annie? There you are. And what are we having for breakfast?" She plopped down onto the empty stool in between the girls.

"Blueberries," Eva said as she crammed one in her mouth.

"Yogurt," Annie said.

"Yum. What kind of yogurt?"

"Cherry."

"Want to see my b-loon?" Eva asked.

"I would love to. Maybe after you're done with breakfast. Okay?"

I watched the conversation from the kitchen doorway. "Poppy, thanks for coming, but I was planning to call a cab. This isn't necessary."

"It's not a problem. I was headed in your direction anyway." She stole a blueberry out of Eva's bowl and popped it in her mouth.

"Hey," my daughter said.

Poppy pulled a face and winked. Eva returned with a giggle.

That had to be a big, fat lie because I knew her townhouse was not in any way, shape, or form near my place. Neither was her office. Nonetheless, it was sweet of her to come. "Can I get you a cup of coffee or something to eat? I need to finish getting dressed. Sanvi should be here in about fifteen, twenty minutes."

She waved me away. "Go get dressed. These young ladies and I can manage, can't we?"

"We sure can." Annie's curls bounced up and down.

Poppy tweaked her nose. I shrugged and headed to my room.

Thirty minutes later as we drove out of the neighborhood, her interrogation began. "So-o … your sister said things looked like they were getting hot and heavy with our sexy detective. You two finally stepping it up?"

I squeezed my eyes shut and pinched the bridge of my nose. "Why, oh why, must I have a nosy sister?"

"Hey, we're only interested because we care."

"I suppose." I sighed.

"That and because we've been watching the two of you circling each other like cats in heat. It's painful to watch. I really thought after the party something would happen. But Sophie said you passed out on the way home."

"Don't remind me." I groaned. "That was a mother of all hangovers."

"Anyway, I'm dying to hear what happened last night."

"Nothing happened last night."

"Nuh-uh. That's not what Sophie said. She said when she got back with the girls, Gary was walking funny. Your hair looked like it'd been styled with an electric mixer, and you had that glazed 'I don't know what hit me,' look about you."

I mashed my lips together.

"So, who's telling the truth—you or Soph?"

"I plead the fifth."

"Forget it. This isn't a courtroom. It's Guantanamo, and if you don't tell me what I want to know, I'm going to torture it out of you."

"Waterboarding? Seems rather drastic."

"I considered it. But I figure all I have to do is fill you with booze and you'll spill your secrets. It's better than sodium pentothal."

The car halted at a stoplight. Poppy turned her big insect glasses on me.

"The light's green."

She didn't move but continued to regard me.

"Time to go."

Someone laid on their horn. Poppy didn't move. Another horn honked.

"*Okay. Fine!* I'll tell you if you'll just *go*."

The car jerked forward. "Talk."

"We were interrupted three different times in the middle of a lip-smacking make-out session. It was awful."

"The kissing or the interruptions?"

"The interruptions."

"Aw, you poor thing. So, is our handsome detective a good kisser?"

"Oh, yes-s," I said with a giant sigh. "It was beyond good."

"Some hidden heat behind that cool exterior."

"To say the least."

"Woohoo!" Poppy's whoop was so loud I jumped at the sound of it in the enclosed vehicle. She pumped a fist in the air. "So, did he stay the night? Did you two do a little couch bouncing once the rug rats went to bed?"

"No," I snapped, then mumbled, "He left right after Sophie."

"Hmm, so where does this leave you two? You finally going to consummate your relationship?"

"*Jesus*, I don't know. We don't really have that kind of relationship."

Poppy burst into laughter. "Are you kidding me? You two are already married in every sense of the word, except sexually. You take care of each other's kids like they're your own. You're always there for each other in times of need. He's at your house all the time.

"That's because of the girls."

"I bet you know what his favorite dish and television shows are."

"Lasagna and *Modern Family.*"

"Does he wear boxers or briefs?"

"Boxer briefs." It slipped out before I could think twice, and I smacked a hand over my mouth.

"See!" She hooted.

"I was out shopping, and he asked if I could pick up a few things for Annie, and …" I shut my trap before I said anything more incriminating. The underwear knowledge was completely, I mean completely, innocent. However, I had a feeling no matter what I said, Poppy would find a way to misconstrue it.

"You two have a passion for each other just shimmering at the surface. Hell, you even bicker like a married couple."

"I don't know what you're talking about. We never bicker."

"Sure you do. At Ian's Christmas bash. You two got into it over our role in the Middle East. You're obviously comfortable with each other. He's your swan."

"Okay, what's up with the waterfowl reference? Sophie said something similar to me the other day."

"It came from my mom. Swans are birds that mate for life. Ian is Sophie's swan, Adam is mine, and Gary is yours."

I blew out a breath. "I think you're getting ahead of yourself. I'm not even sure I should encourage what happened last night to happen again."

"Whyever not?"

"Because I don't think either of us is ready. Gary's wife left him less than a year ago. And I'm not even divorced a full year."

"Pshaw. Both of you have been emotionally detached from your former relationships a lot longer than that."

She had a point.

"And your relationship is different. What started from a mutual need of each other's time and child-rearing skills has moved into a relationship. You're both raising those girls together. Now you just need to open yourself emotionally. You care about him, don't you?"

I nodded.

"Gary sure as hell cares for you."

"Yes, he does. As a *friend*."

She snorted. "Friend my ass. That man watches your every move when you're in the room. Even when he's not watching you, his instincts know where you are at all times. Take Sophie's party. I asked him where you'd gotten to, and he didn't turn his head an inch before saying, 'by the bar talking to Mario.' Sure enough, when I pushed through the crowd, there you were … with Mario. It was uncanny."

"That's just his training."

"Perhaps. But he seems to have it turned on to high alert when you're around." She pulled into Le Pinceau's parking lot and cruised slowly past the broken glass, eyeing the flagging yellow crime scene tape around the car and the plastic over the window that Officer Mahoney had kindly rigged up yesterday. She whistled and stopped the car.

"Well, thanks for the ride." I opened the door, desperate to escape the interrogation.

"Listen, hon." She grabbed my arm. "I know I've been torturing you with questions about Gary, but I want you to know you're not alone."

"I know. I've got Sophie and Ian."

"And me too. I'm a phone call away. I'm not just 'Sophie's friend, Poppy.' I'm 'Holly's friend,' too. Got it?"

Poppy, so rarely serious, made my eyes mist, because she was right. I'd always thought of her as Sophie's friend. My sister's best friend. Even though she'd been helpful and caring during the Omar situation, it never occurred to me to call on her. It was lovely to know I had another girlfriend that I could rely on in my ballpark.

"Thanks. I can always use another friend."

"Anytime. Besides, sometimes it's easier to talk to an unrelated girlfriend about love life things. What might be TMI for your sister is never too much for me! I'm always up for hearing about shirt-ripping, gritty sex." She grinned and I released a giggle. Poppy was one person who could always raise my spirits.

After she left, I brushed excess glass off the driver's seat, and sans rodent—since Mahoney had bagged and tagged the rat—I motored the car to the shop.

Gary phoned as I pulled up to a stoplight.

"Morning," I answered.

"Where are you?"

"Taking my car to the shop. Why? Where are you?"

"On my way out of the office. How did you get your car?"

"Poppy picked me up."

"Listen, I have two things to tell you. First, Holtzman hasn't been back to his home and his car hasn't been found yet."

"Should I be worried?"

"Let's just say be alert. Trey's pranks have been rather childish. But if he's high ..."

"Do you think he realizes you're on to him?"

"Maybe. Maybe not. A neighbor said it's not unusual for him to go on a bender and not come home for days. We're checking his usual haunts. But I don't want you going back to the gallery until we've got a bead on this guy."

"That's fine. I think the car will take up most of my day. My boss told me I had the rest of the week off if I needed it."

"Good. How are you going to get home from the auto body? Do you need me to send someone to come get you?"

"The car rental has a shuttle service. I'll get that organized, then head home."

"Okay, I suppose that will be fine."

"Do you think I should be worried about this guy?"

Gary paused. "Honestly, my gut tells me no. But we can't rule out any of the possibilities. I expected a black and white to have picked him up by now. If they don't find him soon, we may need to look into more serious protection for you."

"Geez, don't mention that to Sophie. She said something yesterday about hiring Ziggy." I sniggered.

My quip met silence.

"Gary?"

"That's not a bad idea."

"Oh, good lord." I rolled my eyes. "No. I'll be safe at home."

"We'll leave it as is. For now. In the meantime, I'm going to have a black and white do a drive-by at the auto body shop. I want to make sure you're not being followed."

"Good idea." *Whatever makes you happy.* Like Gary, I didn't have a gnawing concern in my gut over this guy. So far, his pranks, though certainly annoying, were rather childish. I had a feeling that after his vandalism, Trey was the type to go celebrate. I imagined he'd be crowing about it to his cronies and was either passed out in his car in an alley behind one of the downtown bars or at a flophouse, taking a ride on Puff the Magic Dragon.

"What was the other thing?" I asked.

"Other thing?"

"You said you had two things to tell me. Was it just the stuff about Trey?"

"No, actually I wanted to tell you the latest about Claire. Apparently, she petitioned the court to move up the custody hearing. But my lawyer said it was denied."

"It's still after the New Year, then?"

"So it seems."

"That's good. Right?"

"Yes …"

"What aren't you telling me? You have that tone that says there's something else."

"I just don't understand why she's in a big hurry. Why the petition now? My instincts are buzzing. There's more to this."

I relaxed. Poor Gary was in the middle of this mess, and it would be tough for him to see the big picture. I knew exactly how he felt and I tried to reassure him. "I think she probably wants to see Annie for Christmas. It'll be the first one she's had without her daughter, and that's got to be … devastating."

"If she'd been a normal mother, like you, I'd agree with that statement. However, Claire was never what I would consider overly maternal. It came in waves, and looking back, I'm not sure she has the capability to look outside of herself enough to truly love another person."

"Hmm, I see what you're saying. Perhaps, with the holiday drawing near, it's the first time what she's done has really settled in. I don't think you should read any more into it than that."

A sigh blew across the lines. "Maybe you're right."

"What time will I see you?"

"Normal time. Text me when you've got the rental car and are heading home."

"Will do."

"It's a good possibility I'll get called in tonight. Would it be all right for Annie to spend the night?"

"Of course."

"Thanks. You're the best."

"No prob."

There was an awkward pause. With business now dispensed, I think both of us felt we should address last night's encounter.

"Holly, we should …"

"Listen, I've just …" We spoke at once.

"Sorry," I hurried into the breach. "I've just pulled in and I need to go."

"Right … I guess I'll … um … see you tonight."

"Tonight, then. Since I'll be home, I'm going to cook a nice meal for all of us. Maybe lasagna."

"My favorite. See you later."

I hung up and breathed a sigh of relief.

Chicken. You're going to have to talk about it sometime.

Yes, I know. Just … not right now.

A bell tinkled as I opened the door into the reception area, and I made an effort to focus on the task at hand, dismissing all thoughts of passionate kisses and hard muscular chests.

Yeah, that vow lasted all of ten seconds.

Chapter Eleven

Singing an off-key rendition of "White Christmas," I danced around the steamy kitchen in my tank top as I sprinkled the final layer of cheese on the lasagna, and then stood back to admire my masterpiece. Dirty pots and spatters of sauce littered the counter. The room smelled of tomatoes and garlic. A beep from the oven indicated that it had finished preheating.

The phone rang. "Sanvi, I'm glad you called. I'm home today and I'm making a big batch of lasagna. I plan to send some home with you."

Sniffling came through the lines and a frisson of apprehension shot down my spine.

"Sanvi? Are you okay? What's the matter?"

"They're g-g-gone."

The unease turned to a gut-clenching fear. I gripped the phone tighter. "Who? Sanvi, who's gone?"

The sniveling turned into full-blown sobs.

"Holly?"

"Yes, who is this?"

"This is Joey's mother, Miranda, from Toddler Time."

"I remember."

"I'm so sorry. Sanvi went to the bathroom, and Sam fell off the swings, and we all ran over to him. We took our eyes off the kids for just a moment."

"A moment? What's going on? Miranda, who is gone?"

"The girls."

I sucked wind. "Both of them?"

"Yes."

I flipped the oven off, snatched up my handbag and car keys, and flew out the door. "Maybe they wandered away. They like to play near the creek. Did you check near the creek?"

"Yes, we've looked there. There are about half a dozen parents here looking for them. One of the other moms called 911."

"I'm on my way. I'll be there in ten."

The Chevy's tires squealed as I tore out of the drive and sped off in the direction of the park. I rolled through stop signs, surpassed the speed limit by a good twenty miles an hour, and careened into a space next to a black and white cruiser with its lights flashing. It was the longest eight-and-a-half minutes of my life. The car jerked and the transmission made a grinding sound as I threw it into park before coming to a complete stop. *Good thing it's a rental.* Launching myself out of the vehicle, I took off at a dead run.

"Sanvi!" I hollered. The cop turned, but I ignored her and brushed past to grab Sanvi by the shoulders. "Have they found them?"

Sanvi, red-eyed and gripping a tissue, shook her head. "I'm s-sorry. I was going to t-take them with me to the b-bathroom, but S-sam's mom said she'd keep an eye on them, b-but he fell off the s-swing and ..." The tears started falling again. "I should have taken them with me."

I shook her. "Sanvi. Get a hold of yourself. We need to think. Did anyone else see them?"

She stared at me, uncomprehending.

"Ma'am, ma'am. Please, I was just taking Ms. Nida's statement." The officer stood on my right, but I continued to ignore her.

"Did you call Gary?"

"He d-didn't answer his phone."

I pulled up his number on my cell. It went direct to voicemail. "Gary, it's Holly. It's imperative you call me the second you get this. The girls are gone," I yelled into the phone.

"Ma'am, I need you to calm down."

I finally gave the cop all my attention. "Are you out of your mind? *My daughter is missing* and you expect me to 'calm down'!" I bellowed with hands flapping.

"Ma'am, I understand this is a stressful situation. But I need you to lower your voice and answer a few questions that could help find the little girls." She spoke in a firm voice and stepped aggressively in front of my face.

I drew in a deep breath, clamped down on the panic, and said through gritted teeth, "Are you aware one of those little girls belongs to Detective Gary Sumner of the Van Nuys precinct?"

The officer visibly blanched.

"No? It seems he is unaware that his daughter is missing." I shook the phone at her and lowered my voice. "You need to step off, lady. I am aware you are trying to help. Telling me to calm down is not fucking helping. Finding my daughter would be helpful. Right now, I'm going to take a moment to track down the girl's father and get some real help. Like an AMBER Alert. Have you done that?"

The cop backed down a bit. "We're just about to get that process started. *After* we finish questioning witnesses."

It was at that moment that I noticed another cop talking with other parents who held tight to their own children. The blue and red playground equipment remained empty of happily squealing playfellows. A breeze kicked up and a lone swing shifted, its chains grating against the coupling. A few of the children must have realized something was wrong, their faces frightened as they clung to their parents. A second cop car with lights flashing pulled into the parking lot. Officer Mahoney got out and approached the group of parents.

I dialed the main line for the detective supervisor.

"Alan Grant."

Thank God. "Alan, it's Holly Hartland, again."

"What can I do for you, Holly?"

"Gary's daughter, Annie, and my daughter, Eva, have gone missing and I can't get ahold of him."

"Where are you?"

"At the park." I gave him the address.

"I'll find Sumner and send another detective to you now. Are police on the scene?"

"Yes, I'm here with two black and whites and the cop from yesterday. But I think we might need to send out an AMBER Alert, considering the situation with Trey."

"I'll make sure it gets done." He hung up.

"Ma'am, do you have a picture of either of the girls?" the officer asked.

"Yes, of course. There should be some in my phone." My hands shook as I brought up the photo gallery and searched for a close-up of the girls. The phone sang out.

"Gary?"

"I'm on my way. Are you okay?"

"The girls are gone. I don't know what to do … just … get here." I covered my mouth with a trembling hand. Even so, an agonized whimper escaped.

"I'm coming, sweetheart. I'm coming."

Mahoney and the other officer came up to us.

"One of the moms thought she saw a white sedan parked across the street. But another insisted it was beige, and still another thought it was a silver SUV." Mahoney pointed to an empty parallel parking space by the edge of the grassland. "It may have disappeared about the same time as the girls, but no one saw it leave."

"Where's Sam's mom?" I asked, gazing around the group.

"She took her son to the hospital. He hit his chin pretty hard, knocked out a tooth, and will likely need stitches," the female officer replied.

"Oh." I finally understood why everyone was distracted from the girls. "Did any of the kids see anything?"

The other officer, whose nametag read Branton, shook his head. "Not that is actionable. One of the kids said a purple alien wearing a pink hat took the girls."

That didn't sound promising. The wail of a siren rent the air, and Gary's unmarked cruiser roared on scene. He was out the door like a shot and sprinting across the grass. I met him partway, throwing my arms out. He grabbed me and pulled me tight to his chest.

"Omigod. They're gone. They're gone." I cried into his lapel.

"Shh, shh, it's all right. We're on it. We'll find them." Gary pushed me away and gripped my biceps, I couldn't read his eyes behind his sunglasses, but his jaw remained stiff with tension even as he spoke. "Sweetheart, I need you to be strong. You can't fall apart right now. Okay?"

I gulped back tears and swallowed the hard knot at the back of my throat. "You're right."

He released me and we rejoined the cluster of police. "Word's gone out. They're getting warrants for Holtzman's cell and credit card history. Did anyone see anything?" Gary asked the cops.

They took turns running down what they knew. The nippy breeze biting at my uncovered flesh filtered into my consciousness. In my flight out the door, I'd forgotten to grab a jacket. I rubbed my naked arms in an effort to dispel the goose bumps.

"What about traffic cameras?" Gary asked. Without missing a beat, he removed his sport coat and placed it on my shoulders. The warmth from his body heat leached into me.

"This is a residential neighborhood. No traffic cameras until you get out on the main roads," the lady cop said.

Gary pulled up his phone. "Diana? Gary Sumner. We may have a kidnapping of two young children. I need you to access traffic cam footage within a three-mile radius of this address." He provided the park's address, then returned his attention to the officer. "I want uniforms knocking on doors. See if someone was looking out a window, or has security cameras with a view of the street."

Branton nodded and made notes. The phone rang again. "Sumner. Yes. No. I'm not sure that's necessary ... Yes, I know. This is my daughter we're talking about ... Yes ...Yes, sir." Stiffly he turned to me. "Holly, I need you to return to the house."

"*No.*" My hair brushed my cheeks as I vehemently shook my head. "I need to stay here and help look for them. Maybe they just wandered off ..." I tried to convince myself that the kids were merely lost and looking for me, because the other option was simply too ghastly to contemplate.

"Yes, and we will continue searching. But, considering the situation with Holtzman, it's possible there will be a ransom demand."

"Ransom? Are we sure it's Holtzman? Doesn't it seem a bit of a leap to go from vandalism to kidnapping?" I argued.

"He's a drug addict, and addicts always need money. They are devious, sneaky, and skilled liars. He could have enticed the girls to go with him. And this could be his screwed up way of getting revenge on you."

I crossed my arms and stared mutinously.

"Holly, please." He ran a frustrated hand through his hair. "I need you to return home. The FBI's on the way."

"The FBI? Who called the FBI?"

"It's standard in kidnapping cases."

"Why are they going to my home? Tell them to come here"—I pointed at the ground—"so they can help look."

"They're coming to set up a tap on your home and cell phone. In case ... kidnappers make contact with you."

I chewed my lip, processing that news. "I hear what you're saying. But I can't just leave this park. This is where they were last seen. I *need* to stay and help with the search. After all, we don't even know if they've been taken. How can we be sure they didn't just wander off? Send Sanvi back to the house." I waved my hand toward where Sanvi stood a bit apart from the pack of concerned parents, sniffing and wiping her nose with a tatty tissue. "She can talk to the FBI and wait for the calls."

"Holly." He pulled me away from the assemblage and spoke in firm undertones. "You have to go. If it's not Holtzman, and if they indeed wandered off, someone we know could find them and return the girls to the house. If they show up and are met with FBI agents, they'll get scared. I need you to be there. Just in case. Okay?"

My head bobbed as I considered his words. Gary had a point. "You're right. Maybe one of the neighbors saw them wandering the streets." I snapped my fingers as a new thought occurred. "Or maybe they decided to walk home. I've done it with them once or twice. But we take the bike path that goes through the woods past the Calders' house. I'll bet that's it. Okay, I'll take the path back to the house and call you if I find them on the way." Before I could turn away, Gary stopped me.

"That's a good idea, and I'll have some officers walk the route. But, it's more important for you to go home. Now." Removing his sunglasses, his gaze speared me, and what I read in them gave me an uncomfortable jolt. Gary must have been taking great pains to hide behind his levelheaded façade, because fear swirled like a tempest in the depths of his eyes. They were indeed the windows to his soul.

It finally clicked; he was working on the assumption that they'd been kidnapped. Not wandered off, as I hoped. He needed me to follow directions and not argue. A sob rose in my throat, but I gulped it back with a shaky nod.

Relief flashed. "Take Sanvi to my house. I'm sending a black and white over there in case the girls turn up."

An awful thought came to mind and I blurted out without thinking, "What if it's not Trey? What if it's someone you've put in jail?"

His jaw clenched and his gaze turned to flint. "We're already working that angle. They'll be tapping my phone as well. I'm sending a detective to the studio to question people from Ian's party. Can you call him to let him know? Then I need you to call your sister, just to make sure the girls didn't go off with her."

I dialed as he spoke. "She'd never walk off with the girls without telling someone."

"You'd be surprised what a simple miscommunication can cause," Mahoney interjected.

"Ian's phone."

I was momentarily stymied by the female voice that answered because it wasn't my sister, until I remembered that Ian sometimes gave his phone to his personal assistant. "Brittany?"

"Yes."

"It's Holly Hartland, Sophie's sister. I need to speak with Ian."

"They're in the middle of filming a scene."

"It's an emergency."

"Is Sophie okay?"

"She's fine. My daughter's been kidnapped and Ian might be able to help."

"Omigod. Hang on."

I counted the seconds as I waited.

"Holly? What's going on? Brittany interrupted filming. My director's shitting his trousers."

I could hear an angry male voice in the background chewing Brittany out and telling her she was fired.

"I'm sorry, Ian, but Eva and Annie have been kidnapped. We think it's possible it has something to do with Trey Holtzman." My voice shook. "He hasn't been located yet. Gary's sending a detective over to interview anyone who was at the party and might know more about him."

"Holly, I'm so sorry. I'll gather everyone who was at the party, but so far nobody's confessed to bringing him. We're still not sure how the wanker got in. What else can I do?"

"What you're doing. And pray."

"Have you called Sophie?"

"Not yet. I will when I get off with you."

"I'll do it. Where are you?"

"Heading back to my place. The FBI is coming over in case we get a ransom demand."

"Christ. I'll do what I can from here, and I'm sending Ziggy over. He might be able to help."

"No, wait." But my response met dead air. Gary was having hushed conversations with the other officers. "It's all set with Ian," I told him. "He said he'd gather up anyone who was at the party, and he's calling Soph."

"I need you and Sanvi to call the parents of any of the girls' friends. Anyone you can think of with whom they might walk away without a fuss."

"Most all of their friends were here today," Sanvi said.

"Search your phone's directory. Call everyone." Gary stood with hands on hips, and for a brief moment the ice in his eyes melted as he gazed at me. "Will you be all right to drive home? Do you want one of the officers to take you?"

"No, they need to work with you. I'll be fine. Come on, Sanvi," I said with determination. It wouldn't do the girls any good if I fell apart right now.

Chapter Twelve

Once we climbed in the rental car, Sanvi started to speak, but I silenced her with a hand. Even though I knew it was unreasonable, anger had joined fear, and I wasn't willing to rant at her only to regret it a few hours from now. Rationally, I realized it could have happened to anyone. I'd offered on occasions to watch another mother's child while she went to the bathroom. It was the network we'd created. Everyone watched out for each other's kids. Except today. Everyone was paying attention to Sam, while my two were snatched right out from under their noses. Sanvi must have understood my mood and instead turned her attention to phoning parents.

At a stop sign, I realized I'd been gripping the steering wheel so hard my knuckles had gone white, but I didn't dare loosen them because I was afraid if I did, the shaking would start and become uncontrollable.

Gary's driveway stood empty; no sign of a police car, yet. "Come on, Sanvi, let's check inside." *Maybe the girls found their way home.*

"Girls? Eva? Annie?" My voice echoed through the house.

Sanvi headed up the stairs to the bedrooms, calling the girls, while I went to the back door, flipped the lock, and headed into the backyard. My voice floated across the silent yard. I checked behind the overgrown bushes beside the house and walked the fence line. Nothing.

Sanvi opened and closed cabinets in the kitchen as I shut the door behind me.

"Anything?"

She shook her head.

"You check the laundry room?"

"Not there." The cabinet closed with a snap.

"They're not here, are they?"

She mashed her lips together and her obsidian eyes glassed over with tears.

I rubbed a hand down my face and sighed. "Okay. Stay here. A police officer will be here soon. I've got to get back to my house to meet the FBI. Call me if you hear anything."

She used a sleeve to wipe her nose. If I had been a good person, I would've comforted her. Told her it would all be okay, and that it wasn't her fault. Told her to stay strong, that we'd find the girls. I must not have been a good person. I was barely holding my own shit together, and right now it wasn't in me to comfort the person who lost my child. It was her fault, and I did blame her. I shut Gary's door without a backward glance.

A black SUV sat in front of my house; two men in dark suits, white shirts, nondescript ties, and sunglasses got out as I pulled into the driveway.

"Are you Mrs. Hartland?" The balding, older man removed his glasses as he spoke.

"Yes. FBI?"

"I'm Agent Black and this is Agent Martin." He pointed to the young, dark-haired, bearded agent behind him.

"Can I see your IDs, please?"

Agent Black dug into his coat pocket while Martin sighed and I swear rolled his eyes behind his shades before digging out his badge. Sure enough, Roland Black and Matthew Martin, FBI agents. Roland seemed like a seasoned agent, but Martin's photo must have been taken before the beard and showed a young, unlined face. *Great, they've sent in a trainee.*

"Come in. I understand you're going to be tapping my phones in case I get a ransom demand."

"That is correct, ma'am. We'll be coordinating efforts with the local police," Black said.

As my key slipped into the lock, another large, black SUV rolled up behind the FBI's; the door popped open and Ziggy heaved his body out.

"Who's that?" Martin tensed and put his hand on his hip. It reminded me of Gary.

"Relax, Junior, he's a friend." I waved at Ziggy and pushed open the door.

The scent of garlic and tomatoes still filled the air, but it felt like hours ago that I'd been humming happily, making tonight's dinner rather than … fifty minutes. *Has it really been fifty minutes?* I went directly to the kitchen with the two agents and Ziggy following behind, like a drum major leading the parade.

The answering machine's light stayed a constant red, not blinking to reveal a waiting voicemail. I don't know what I'd been expecting—perhaps hoping against hope that a friendly neighbor had found the girls harmlessly wandering the streets. That solid red light disheartened me, and the room started to spin. Anxiety clawed at the back of my throat. I stumbled backward against a solid body.

"Mrs. Hartland. Are you okay?"

The voice came from far away and the edges of my vision darkened. Hands wrapped around me and guided me to a chair.

Voices spoke, blending together. "Is she okay?" "What's wrong with her?" "Get some water."

Agent Black's face swam through my vision, and I could see his mouth moving, but the buzzing in my ears drowned out whatever he said. His face suddenly disappeared and icy water drenched my face, slamming me back to the present as effectively as if I'd been slapped. The ringing dissipated.

"What the *hell?*" I sputtered and swiped at the liquid.

"Are you okay?" Ziggy crouched in front of me, gently blotting at my face with a dishtowel. "You were having a panic attack or something."

I took the towel from him and wiped my eyes. "Who's the joker that threw the water?"

Ziggy shifted to reveal Agent Martin standing with an empty glass gripped at his side. Black, with a warning look, held a restraining hand against his colleague's shoulder. Martin, unperturbed, shrugged.

I gave him the evil eye, then turned back to Ziggy. "Sorry. I don't know what came over me."

"Are you okay now?"

"Yes. I'm fine."

His meaty paw patted my back and helped to my feet. "Why don't you go change into something dry while the feds do their business?"

I removed Gary's sodden coat and hung it on the back of the chair, then tossed my cell phone on the table for the FBI. The moment the bedroom door closed behind me, brainwaves of fear exploded in all directions, tumbling over each other like newborn pups fighting for their mother's teat. The worst thoughts I held at bay, refusing to give life to them as I numbly changed with shaking hands into a fresh pair of jeans and a sweatshirt. I washed my face free of the smudged make-up and stared in the mirror.

"Get ahold of yourself. They're going to be okay," I whispered in a wobbly voice. "Gary will find them. They're going to be fine." I breathed deeply, then said in a firm voice, "They're going to be *fine." They'll be fine. They'll be fine.* The hopeful mantra spun in my head, and I clasped my hands together to stop the shaking.

I'm not normally a religious person, and it had been years since I'd seen the inside of church. I'd kind of given up on God after my father dropped dead from a brain aneurysm, leaving my mother a widow in her fifties. Nevertheless, I dropped down, my knees hitting the porcelain tile hard enough to leave bruises, and sent prayers up to God. I begged him to return the girls home safely. I bargained with the Almighty, promising to go to church every

Sunday, promising to be a better person, promising never again to yell at my child, promising to keep the house clean, promising to help the homeless—mindless promises reeled through my whispering lips, if only he would return my babies to me … alive.

I don't recall how long I remained in the penitent position, my forehead resting against my clenched fingers, when a deep voice resonated through the bathroom, interrupting my babbling prayers. *"Get up."*

The words were simple and straightforward and clear as a bell. My eyes flew open, and I tilted my head—listening.

"Hello?"

No one was in the bathroom, my bedroom door remained closed, and I could hear the murmur of male voices coming from the other part of the house. Nobody was with me and yet … I could have sworn the voice sounded like my father's. *Impossible.* The memory of the voice still echoed around me.

I didn't know if it was God, my dad, or my own subconscious speaking, but that voice got me off the floor, allowed me to clear my head, and helped me march down the hall with a determined stride.

I found Agent Black sitting at the kitchen island, phone to his ear, scratching away on a notepad. Ziggy leaned against the counter, watching and listening with narrowed eyes. The FBI had set up shop at the dining room table. Hard, black cases filled with unidentifiable electronics sat open, and Agent Martin had my cell hooked up to a laptop.

"What are you doing?"

"Downloading your texts and call history for the past week," he said without looking up from the computer.

"I don't believe I gave you permission to do that," I snapped. I knew I was being unreasonable. But I was angry and frightened and still irritated over the dousing. Junior seemed to be an easy target to take my frustrations out on.

"It may help us find your daughter." He continued tapping on the keyboard without missing a beat, unfazed by my rudeness.

I walked away before any more sharp comments slipped out. As I stared into the backyard, all I could think about was yesterday when the girls ran with Sanvi and Sirius. Giggling. Safe. Home.

Spinning away from the window, I erased the mental picture. The kitchen, still a disaster from my earlier efforts, caught my attention. Unsure what to do next, I attacked the mess like a demon, scouring and scrubbing with utter concentration as though my life depended upon it. At some point, Ziggy went out back; I saw him pacing and talking on his phone. Agent Black's voice droned in the background as I cleaned, but I didn't process the conversation.

"Mrs. Hartland, you want to tell us about this?"

Startled, I looked up from the stain on the stove top I'd been scraping with my fingernail to find Agent Black holding up a piece of paper.

My brows knit in confusion. "What's that?"

He passed it over and the handwriting leaped out at me. I dropped the hateful letter as one would a black widow spider. "Who said you could open my mail? I believe it's a federal offense opening someone else's mail."

"It was sitting out," Martin said from his position at the dining table.

"Bullshit." I spit out.

"Mrs. Hartland, we're just trying to help here." Black pressed a finger to his temple. "This is what we call a lead. What can you tell me about the letter?"

"It's from my ex-husband's father. They lost a bid for custody of Eva, and his belligerence with the judge also lost them visitation rights since the divorce. That is my monthly hate mail."

"And you didn't think to mention this to anyone?"

"It … it … slipped my mind. Besides, Trey …" *Omigod. Was Agent Black right? Could Omar's parents have taken the girls, not Trey?*

"Where is your husband?"

"Ex-husband. He's in San Quentin."

"Let's confirm that. Matt, follow up on the grandparents. Do you have phone numbers? Where do they live?"

"On the East Coast. Junior has my cell phone. You'll find them under Rashid, but I can't imagine they'd kidnap both the girls. Maybe Eva, but why would they take Annie? They don't even know her."

"No witnesses." Martin mumbled.

That one hit me dead center in the solar plexus. My knees went weak, and I grabbed at the counter to keep from collapsing on the hardwood floor.

Black shot a look at his subordinate just as his phone rang. "Agent Black. Yes, yes, uh-huh, are they sure? Did the alibi check out? …Yes … Uh-huh … Well, you might want to get over here. We have a new lead …. The grandparents, there was a letter. We're following it up now." He hung up and looked at me. "Holtzman has been found."

"And."

The agent's bald pate shook back and forth. "He's been on a bender in San Diego since yesterday. He confessed to vandalizing your car, but he didn't kidnap the girls. Witnesses alibied him out."

With a snap of a finger, the situation took an even more sinister turn. My hands fisted at my sides, and I forced down the bile that rose in my throat.

"What about the bike path? Has anyone walked the path?"

The agent nodded. "K-9 units walked the path both ways. Nothing."

I scrunched my eyes shut. *Keep it together. Keep it together.*

An instant later, my feet pounded down the hall into my room. Whipping open the walk-in closet, I grabbed the blue and white shoebox that held all of the unopened letters from the Rashids. Other boxes displaced and fell to the floor, scattering shoes willy-nilly, but I ignored them, instead returning to mission control. I plunked the box on the table at Agent Martin's elbow.

"These are all the letters I've received this past year. I ... stopped opening them after a while."

The two agents eyed the box. Black lifted his chin at me. "Thanks, this will help."

"Junior, do what you have to—search my mail, phone records, email, trash, Tampax box, whatever." I looked at him with pleading eyes. "Find my girls."

He scrutinized me with an unreadable face. "The name's Matt."

"I'm sorry. Matt," I mumbled, sinking into a seat at the table. "Please, just find my girls."

His jaw softened. "Doing my best, ma'am ... and I'm sorry about the water."

"S'okay. Call me Holly."

He gave a sharp nod. "Holly, I doubt we'll need to search the Tampax, but these letters will be a good start."

Black went out the front door with a cell phone glued to his ear. I rocked back and forth, and the only sound to be heard was ripping paper as Matt opened the letters. His frown deepened as he read each one.

Suddenly, the door opened and slammed and Gary strode into the house. Flinty-eyed, he snatched up the letter at the top of the neat pile Matt had made.

"Hey," Matt started to protest, but one look at the gun on Gary's hip and his barely banked fury, and he shut his mouth.

Gary's jaw turned to hard granite as his gaze swept down the page. "I thought we agreed you would pass these on to me if you received any more." A harsh, unrecognizable voice grated against my ears as he shook the offensive letter at me.

I rose. "I don't recall agreeing to that. Besides, I didn't think it was a big deal." As the words fell out of my mouth, I knew they were wrong on so many levels, and the acid rolling in my gut cranked up a notch.

"You. Didn't. Think. It. Was. A. Big. *Deal!*" His fist smashed the table and I flinched. "Our girls are missing, and you didn't think it was a good idea to bring these vitriol-filled letters to my attention?"

"You thought it was Trey Holtzman," I said in an unsteady voice and moved behind the chair to put further distance between us.

"Clearly it's not. You withheld vital information that could help us find the girls!"

"I'm sorry. I thought it was Trey." The placating voice came naturally, a throwback from my days in Las Vegas. "When the FBI suggested it could be someone besides Trey, I brought them the information immediately. I'm sorry. Don't be angry."

"I should have known about this before *today.* We talked about this! This is beyond irresponsible!" His wrath came at me like a tidal wave. I'd never seen Gary lose his temper, and the fact that I'd made him this angry scared the shit out me. Omar's pinched, anger-filled face flashed in my mind's eye, and I shrank from it.

Matt rose and left the room.

My eyes darted to his retreating back. *Omigod! Don't leave!*

"Damn it, Holly, stop cowering! I'm not going to hit you!" Gary bit out and fisted his hands on his hips. "What the hell were you thinking? You're messing with my child's life."

"It's my child, too! How do you know this isn't some scumbag you put away?" Like a snake backed into a corner I struck out to defend my indefensible actions. I pointed an accusing finger at him, and my voice went from placating to shriek faster than a

Ferrari at the Indy 500. "How dare you lay all the blame at my feet? How do we even know this is about *me*? Why can't it be about *you*! I'm sure there's a line out the door from your days in homicide. Anyone get out of jail recently? And what about your batshit, crazy ex-wife? Anyone know where Claire is?"

Gary's stare changed to slits. I knew I was pushing the envelope bringing up Claire, but the words continued to tumble out unheeded. "Maybe she decided to take the girls to Disneyland with her latest Euro-trash boy-toy!"

"All right, that's enough," Agent Black's voice thundered across our argument. "Playing the blame game helps no one, and we'll end up right back here where we are. Understood?" He and Agent Martin looked ready to grab one or both of us should the argument turn physical.

The front door burst open, breaking the palpable tension. All heads turned.

"*Holly?*" my sister's voice rang out. She came around the corner, and, spotting me, pushed past all the men to envelop me in a crushing embrace. "Are you okay?"

The dam that I hadn't fully realized I'd been holding back burst open, and full-on, soap opera-style sobbing commenced. It included teeth-rattling shakes and incoherent blubbering of my unspoken fears. At some point, Sophie led me to the couch in the family room and rocked me as the tears tumbled forth. After a while, I ran out of steam and the waterworks slowed to hiccupping whimpers. My chest and throat rattled as I breathed, raspy and sore from the exertion.

A freckled hand held a tissue box in front of me.

"Forgive me. I'm sorry I lost my temper. The girls … I just …" Gary's face was drawn, contrite.

Hot embarrassment flooded my cheeks. I'd been allowed this useless breakdown while Gary, in the same boat as I, was probably using all his mental efforts to keep it together. He'd had every right to blast me for keeping those notes a secret. I'd been foolish to ignore them and keep them hidden, knowing from the first that Gary just wanted to protect me.

"I know." I nodded, blowing my nose. "I shouldn't have kept the letters from you."

Someone called his name and he squeezed my shoulder before returning to base camp. Ziggy stood in a corner, arms crossed, patiently waiting for the waterworks to subside.

Ashamed that he'd witnessed my utter loss of control, I said, "Ziggy, I think we have enough help. You don't have to stay."

"Tell me about Claire." He uncrossed his arms and lowered himself on the ottoman; the cushion collapsed completely beneath his weight.

Sophie took the lead, explaining the Claire situation, and I interjected at intervals to clarify.

"Where is she living now?"

I shrugged. "Gary said something about a marina. Boat slip? I'm not really sure."

Dialing his phone, Ziggy disappeared into the other room, and I commenced to clean myself up with half a box of tissues. When he returned, I had regained a modicum of control and dispatched the snarbly nose.

"I have some contacts in the area. I'm going to step out for a bit to see what I can find," he said.

"What is it?" I asked.

"Nothing specific … just a gut feeling." He pulled a set of keys out of his pocket.

Agent Black and Gary returned to the room.

"I'm not clear who you are or what your role is here," Black said.

"Just a helpful friend." Ziggy pulled a card out of his back pocket and handed it to the agent.

Having seen his card myself last year, I knew it identified him as Kaihe Zigarelli, investigative and security services.

Gary eyed Ziggy but said nothing.

"So, you're a PI," Black stated in a slightly disgusted voice.

Ziggy's gaze remained impassive.

"He also provides bodyguard services. He was very helpful last year when Holly's ex-husband followed her to town ..." Sophie trailed off, thankfully realizing that she may not be helping.

"We're running a controlled investigation here. I don't need a maverick out on his own, getting in the way," Black said.

"Have you had a ransom demand yet?" Ziggy asked.

The agent remained mute.

"Not getting in anyone's way. I'm just going to ask a few people some questions. Put my ear to the ground."

"You might inadvertently put the children in danger. What's your plan?" Black asked.

His shoulders rose up and down. "Like I said, going to ask a few people some questions. Folks who won't be likely to speak to anything that even smells of law enforcement." His face remained neutral.

The light bulbs came on. Black's frown deepened while Gary's actually lightened.

"I think we ought to let Ziggy ask his questions, with the caveat that he keep us informed should he come across any viable tips." Gary continued to study Ziggy as he spoke.

Ziggy made a big X across his chest. "Cross my heart, gentlemen. I only want to get the girls home."

The agent continued to give him the stink eye.

"Black, I think I've got something," Matt's voice called from mission control.

"Fine. Keep us in informed of what you're doing." The agent gave a sharp nod and exited.

"Be careful, Ziggy," Gary said before following the agent.

I rose and walked Ziggy to the door. "Do whatever you can," I whispered. "Whatever it takes. You get me? Find them. Money is no object."

He nodded and left.

I returned to mission control to find more suits. I guess they arrived while I was having my breakdown. *Fabulous. How many people saw my stage-worthy performance?* Glancing around, I mentally identified the feds from local PD: four feds, all in dark suits that looked like they came straight off a Brooks Brothers rack. LAPD wore brown or gray sport coats that looked like they came from JCPenney. A few had removed their jackets and rolled up their sleeves, including Gary.

As far as I was concerned, the more people looking for the girls, the better.

• • •

Gary studied Holly over one of the hate letters he'd been reading. Her eyes, still red, were clear of tears and she spoke in a firm voice. No more cringing fear. The shaking had also stopped. She wore a black sweatshirt with the Nike swoosh across the front, and her face, though still blotchy from crying, held a determined look.

"Have you found the Rashids?" she asked no one in particular.

"They weren't home." Agent Black looked up from his tablet. "We have people knocking on neighbors' doors to see if anyone knows where they are."

"Can you check their phone records? Credit cards?" she pressed.

"Working on that now," Gary responded. Guilt over his loss of temper with her remained in the background and would eventually eat at him. But not now. Right now, he had to concentrate on the task at hand, because he knew statistically that every hour that passed made the chances of finding his girls alive lower. Right now, he existed on his training, going through the steps, working with the other detectives and feds. He buried the frustrated, angry, animalistic yell he longed to release. There would be time for that. Later. Not now.

"Why don't you go lie down and rest? Let us take care of this Mrs. Hartland," one of the feds suggested. Gary had forgotten his name.

"I'm not an invalid or a senior citizen. It's the middle of the day. I don't need a *damn* nap. I need to know what's going on with this investigation to find my kids," she retorted. "And it's Ms. Hartland not Mrs. I'm not married."

The young agent who had been here when Gary arrived gave a snort.

Good. The tough and resilient Holly has returned. Gary gave a slight shake of his head before returning to the letter in his hand. Everyone else went back to whatever they were doing and proceeded to ignore her. She pulled out a chair and plopped herself next to the snorter.

"Matt, you find anything in my emails that can help?" she asked.

"Not yet."

She looked around, but no one else would meet her gaze. "You seem kind of young to be an agent. Are you one of those prodigy kids? What's your background?" Her questions came out in short bursts.

Matt stopped typing and turned to her. "I have an IT degree. Joined the FBI after graduation."

Without glancing up from his phone, Black interjected, "He's being modest. Matt graduated summa cum laude from MIT. We recruited him his junior year because his computer skills are top notch. If there's an electronic footprint from the Rashids, Matt will find it. You're working with one of the best, ma'am."

She let out a breathy sigh and tapped her nails on the table. "What can I do?"

"Wait. Let us do our job." Matt looked pointedly at her tapping fingers.

She whipped them off the table, tucking them under her thighs, which soon began bouncing, jiggling the entire table. The agent glanced up at Gary, and ever so slightly tilted his head in her direction.

"Holly, why don't you come with me, and I'll give you an update of what we're doing. Would that make you feel better?"

"Yes! Thank you." She jumped up, and taking her by the hand, he led her into the living room where he found Sophie speaking in low tones on her cell.

"That would be great. You're a doll. Thanks." She hung up. "Poppy's coming over. She's picking up Chinese on the way. Oh, and I talked with Mom. She's arranging to get a flight out as soon as possible."

Holly blanched, whether at the mention of food or the news about her mother, Gary wasn't sure.

"I know. But you'll need to eat at some point. To keep up your strength," Sophie said.

"Wait a minute. You called Mom? She's coming out?"

"Yes, of course. Gary asked me to do it. She was coming on Christmas Eve anyway. Now she'll come a few days early."

Holly whipped around, but he cut her off before she could speak. "It's procedure. I told you to contact everyone you knew who the girls might get in the car with."

"Did you call your parents?"

"Yes, of course."

She flopped down on the sofa and deflated like a balloon. "Everybody better hang onto their hats. Dorothy Hartland is coming."

Sophie patted her thigh. "I know she can be a lot to take. But, she's our mom, and now is the time for family to be here for you. Besides, how do you think she'd feel, pacing the house alone, waiting for news? She's Eva's grandmother. She deserves to know what's going on."

"I'm sorry. You're right." Holly pressed against her eyes.

Gary laid a hand on her shoulder. "Are your parents coming, too?" she asked shaking his hand off as she turned.

"Not yet. But if we don't hear anything in the next twenty-four hours, there will be little I can say to keep them away."

The three of them went silent, lost in their own thoughts. Someone had turned on the Christmas tree, and he contemplated the colored lights. Only five days until Christmas, and his little girls were missing. It had been a long while since he'd been to church, but as he stared at the tree, a prayer for their safe return ran through his head.

Remembering the original purpose for removing Holly from the hubbub of the dining room, he said, "We have search parties in the park. And we're following up on the Rashids. Detectives are combing my files."

"Has someone checked your house?" Sophie asked.

"Sanvi's there." They both spoke at once.

"I went there after I left the park, and we've got a unit there now," Gary clarified. "But since I don't have a house phone, it's more likely any sort of ransom demand will come to the landline here, or one of our cell phones."

"Are you still expecting a ransom demand, even though Trey's been cleared?" Sophie asked.

Gary shrugged. "It's a possibility we can't rule out."

"Have you spoken with Claire?" Holly gave him a frosty glance.

"I haven't been able to contact her. The cell number she gave me is turned off."

"What about the address she gave you?"

"We're working on it."

"Could she have done this?" Sophie asked with a skeptical face.

He scrubbed a hand through his hair. He hadn't put too much manpower on the search for Claire, concerned that this kidnapping could be used against him in her bid for custody. "No. First, I don't think she'd be smart enough to pull off a stunt like this. Second, why would she take Eva, too? She doesn't even know Eva."

Sophie nodded, accepting his explanation, but Holly's expression didn't seem to be quite as certain.

"Don't worry. We're following every lead we can. We're putting a lot of effort into the Rashid angle right now."

Holly jumped up and started pacing in front of the coffee table. "It's driving me crazy not doing anything. I feel useless. There's got to be something I can do. Walk the neighborhood. Search the park. Make copies of their picture and go door to door." She pounded her fist into her palm.

"We're already doing that," Gary assured her.

"Sweetie, everyone is doing what they can. You need to be here in case there's a phone call," Sophie said.

"What if there's no phone call?" Holly whispered hollowly.

"There will be. Or the police will find them. I have faith." Sophie got up and hugged her sister tight.

Holly remained mute. Chewing her bottom lip, she turned away from her sister to stare at the tree, her shoulders hunched. Somebody called his name, but Gary hesitated, struggling to come up with the right words. To provide some relief. His heart wasn't in it, and none came to mind. Agent Black called his name again and he exited the room in frustration.

Chapter Thirteen

Time passed. I couldn't say if it was slowly or quickly. My body went through the motions, but it felt like I wasn't actually an active participant. After breaking down all over my sister, I couldn't seem to feel. It was almost as though I watched myself from afar, like in a play. Something would come up on the radar and there would be a flurry of activity. Hurried conversations were held. People came and left. Leads were chased down.

Then there were the times when nothing happened, and I would pace through the quiet rooms, my mind blank. Inane ideas would pop into my head, like the fact that the bathtub needed re-caulking. After sunset, the winds picked up and the kitchen screen rattled intermittently. Something else I should get fixed.

The Rashids had left the country and arrived in Morocco five days ago, apparently right after sending their lovely bit of hate mail. Detectives and FBI agents dug deeper into Gary's files, going back to his time as a uniformed officer. Phones rang, but no ransom demands came in.

My dining room occupants had been reduced to Agent Martin, who searched traffic camera footage on his computer and waited with me for a possible ransom call. Nobody said anything, but I knew as time passed, it was less and less likely a call would come in. The police detectives had scattered to follow up other leads. Once the Rashids were cleared, Gary had returned to the precinct to add another set of eyes to comb through his files. So far, nothing. As the night wore on, the only thing that provided any relief was knowing that cops took care of their own, which meant Gary's department was scattered far and wide working all the angles.

Take-out Chinese boxes and mugs littered the dining room table, kitchen island, and living room coffee table. The house smelled of teriyaki sauce and burnt coffee. The living room housed a napping Poppy, while the television quietly hummed in the background. Hours ago, the sun had set, and even though the clock on the cable box now read 2:37, every light in the house burned bright against the darkness.

Sophie leaned against the island, madly texting as I wandered into the kitchen.

"Ian?" I asked.

She nodded, keeping her eyes on the screen. Around ten, she announced Ian would be coming over. An hour later she received a text and told me "he'd been held up." I assumed it was at the studio. I had no idea how much of the cast and crew's time the police had taken up, but since Ian had yet to arrive, it must have been quite a few hours.

I gathered up half-drunk coffee cups, dumped the dregs down the drain, and piled them in the dishwasher.

"Everything okay at the studio?" I asked her.

Her head popped up and she shot me a confused look. Her mouth opened to speak, and then her eyes slid to Agent Martin before returning to me. "Uh, yes … they are just filming some … night shots."

"Soph, do you think the girls are …" The horrible thought stuck in my throat, and I put a hand to my heart.

"No." She vehemently shook her head. "No. I don't. Don't say it. Don't even think it. We will find them."

The sureness of her words re-inflated the hope that had begun to dim in my heart as the hours lengthened.

Her phone chirped and she went back to texting. I shrugged off her strange behavior, contributing it to the lateness of the hour, and returned to the living room. Flopping down on the club chair, I stretched my feet across the ottoman. The heels of my hands scrubbed at my raw, tired eyes, and I closed them to relieve the stinging soreness.

"Holly."

A hand shook my shoulder and I jerked out of light sleep. "What's wrong?"

"Nothing," Sophie whispered. "Let's go for a walk and get some fresh air."

I frowned. *What?* Poppy remained curled up under a blanket, lightly snoring on the couch. The tree lights still twinkled, but the television had been turned off, along with most of the lights in the house. Out of my periphery I could see illumination still shining in the dining room.

"C'mon, Holly. I think you could use some fresh air."

Her stare could only be described as … intense, and my still-sleepy brain wasn't computing.

"What time is it?" I stretched and yawned.

"Five thirty."

"Has there been any news?"

She shook her head.

"I'll make us some fresh coffee."

"Let's go to Starbucks and get some. I'm getting cabin fever, aren't you?" She continued to speak in a whisper so as not to wake Poppy.

"I'm not sure I can leave."

"It's not a problem. I already spoke to Agent Martin. He thought it was a good idea for you to get out for a bit."

"Really? He said it was okay?"

Sophie mashed her lips together and shoved my coat at me.

Well, if the FBI says it's okay… I lumbered out of the chair and shoved my arms into the coat. I noticed she'd tucked my wallet into one of the pockets.

"Agent Martin, you've got my number. Call us if anything develops," Sophie said on our way out.

Without looking up, he waved in our general direction.

The blast of cool air cleared the cobwebs of sleep away, but we had already walked past her CR-V before it registered.

"Hey, aren't we taking your car? Mine's blocked in by Poppy's."

"Just, um, follow me. Ian's picking us up. He said he'd meet us at the corner."

Why the heck couldn't Ian turn the dang corner and drive three houses down? I groused silently, being too emotionally drained and physically exhausted to argue.

We turned the corner and found a large black SUV idling. Sophie opened the back door and I followed her in. "Hey, this isn't Ian's …"

Ziggy sat in the driver's seat and Ian in the passenger's. Talk radio played in the background. Both faces stared at me.

"How are you holding up, luv?" Ian asked.

"Fine … what's going on?"

Eyes darted around, but nobody spoke.

"What's. Going. On?" I repeated slowly and then zeroed in on my sister.

"Ziggy has a hunch."

"Buckle up." Ziggy shifted the car in gear and motored down the street.

A spark of hope ignited in my chest.

"Really? What is it? Wait, I'll call Gary and put him on speakerphone." I fumbled in my pockets, searching for my phone. No such luck. My mind's eye pictured it sitting on the dining room table, next to Agent Martin. "Someone give me a phone. The FBI is still holding mine hostage."

Nobody moved to accommodate me.

"Hey, guys. Phone?"

Ziggy and Ian remained silent, their gazes intent on the street in front of them.

Sophie grimaced as I pegged her with a slit-eyed stare. "We don't want to tell Gary … yet."

"Why not?"

"I'm not sure what I've found. The situation is tenuous, and there's a high possibility things could go wrong if law enforcement is brought into it," Ziggy said.

I gulped. "You mean the girls could be killed by the kidnappers?"

Ziggy shook his head. "Nothing like that. I have a lead, but if the feds get called in, the kidnappers could disappear before we have chance to catch them."

"Them? Do you think you and Ian can handle the kidnappers alone?"

Ian and Ziggy exchanged a look. "Yes, we believe so."

"Look, guys, no offense, I'm sure Ziggy could handle just about anything. But, Ian, come on, you're not a cop. You only play one on TV. You do realize that, right?"

Ian's shoulders shook and I'm pretty sure I heard a snicker. I turned to my ally. "Sophie, come on. Don't you agree we should phone the police? This all seems a little fudgy to me. If you think you have a legitimate lead, we need to call in the cavalry." I poked Ziggy's shoulder. "You promised Agent Black you would keep him apprised of your investigation."

The only reaction Ziggy's profile revealed was the flicker of clenched jaw muscles.

"Bad Boys, Bad Boys," the theme song for the reality show *Cops,* sang out, interrupting the silence.

Sophie pulled her phone from her purse. "It's Gary." She painfully gripped my forearm speaking with quick intensity, "Tell him we're taking you out for breakfast. Please, Holly, for the sake of the girls, don't tell him about Ziggy's lead," and slapped the phone in my hand.

"Hello," I answered.

"Sophie?"

"No, it's me. Holly."

"Hi." There was a pause. "Where are you? Agent Black said you were going out for coffee. But your car is still at the house. So is Sophie's."

"Ian picked us up. They're … taking me out to get something to eat. How are things on your end? Anything to report?"

Gary's sigh whispered across the lines. "Not yet."

"Are you still at the precinct?"

"Yes. My eyes are going cross-eyed from reading these files. I feel as though the key is in here. I'm missing something and it's driving me nuts."

He sounded exhausted and his frustration pulled at my heart. I raised my brow, but Sophie shook her head.

"How are you doing?" he asked.

"Hanging in there … I guess." I bit my tongue to keep from blurting out what I knew.

"It's good you're getting something to eat. Where are they taking you?"

My eyes darted around the car. "Uh, I'm not sure. Let me ask Soph." I put my hand against the speaker and whispered, "He wants to know where we're eating."

Ian threw out the name of a bistro about fifteen minutes away from my place.

I repeated it to Gary. "Why don't you take a break and get a bite to eat, too? Maybe you'll find something with fresh eyes."

"I'll do that. Talk to you later."

"Later." I hung up and threw the phone at my sister. It bounced off her chest and landed on the floor. "I hate lying to him. And I hate being put in a position where I have to. So *someone* better start talking and tell me exactly what the *hell is going on*."

"Boys, tell her," Sophie snapped as she fished around the floorboards.

"Swing by that McDonald's up ahead—we can get some take away and a cup of java. I think we are going to need it," Ian said before shifting in his seat to face me. "Ziggy put the word out on the street about the girls' disappearance. We've spent the night visiting some of the more dodgy sections of town. A little over an hour ago, one of his contacts called with a possible sighting. We're headed there now."

"Who's this contact? Where are we headed?"

"To a marina in Long Beach."

"Long Beach? Who's the contact? The harbormaster?"

"No. It's a man who … deals with … sensitive materials."

"Sensitive materials? I don't get it." I blinked. "You mean like antiques and breakables?"

"Not exactly," Ian said.

"You mean like government documents—is he a spy or something? A CIA spook?" I envisioned Daniel Craig as James Bond.

"No, not anything like that." Ziggy turned into the McDonald's drive-thru.

"Then what?"

Nobody spoke.

"Oh for crying out loud, it's a drug smuggler," Sophie blurted.

"A drug smuggler?" I exclaimed.

"Yes," Ian nodded, "so you can see why we are hesitant to bring this to the … cops' attention."

"My contact said he saw the girls heading out to sea at sunset," Ziggy replied, wheeling the car into the parking lot.

"Sunset!" I slumped against the seat. "That was hours ago. And we're only finding out about this now?"

"Took a while for him to check his messages. He was … busy."

"Busy making a drug shipment," I mumbled, crossing my arms and staring out the window.

Ziggy pulled up to the speaker, and the boys ordered coffee, sodas, and what seemed to me a mountain of breakfast fare. I took the coffee but waved off the food.

The sky began pre-dawn lighting, turning from black to dirty gray, eventually pinking by the time we pulled into the marina. Everyone slipped on sunglasses as the sky brightened; Ian passed me a spare pair of aviators he found in the glove box.

"Wait here." Ziggy turned off the ignition and climbed out

Three pairs of eyes followed his vast body as it lumbered down one of the docks until he disappeared from sight.

"So, have we figured out who owns the boat the girls 'might' have been seen on?" I asked.

"Breisacher, Gaetano Breisacher," Ian replied.

Did that name seem familiar? I shook my head. I'd never even heard of the name Gaetano. What kind of name was that anyway? Italian? Greek?

Ten minutes later, Ziggy reappeared and climbed back in the SUV. "One of the Dana Point marinas sent a mechanic out on a towboat to the *Ulysses* about thirty miles off the coast. It was having engine problems and was dead in the water about four hours ago. Sounds like it might be the one we're looking for."

"Did you get the keys?" Ian asked.

Ziggy held up a key dangling from a foam float that had the Bacardi logo across it. "The boat's clean and doesn't need to be back for seventy-two hours. We're good to go."

"Go? Go where? Shouldn't we call in the Coast Guard or something?" I chimed in.

Ziggy gazed out the front windshield. "The yacht belongs to a German diplomat. My information relies upon a drug dealer who won't speak to the cops and 'thinks he might have seen the girls out of the corner of his eye.' Which means he saw them. If the FBI believed my story, they'd likely have to tell the State Department, and who knows if they would even make a move. Diplomats have immunity. It would be best if we checked it out before calling it in."

"German diplomat? What the hell would a German diplomat want with the girls? Is this some sort of human trafficking ring we're dealing with, Ziggy?"

"No. It's my understanding Claire's boyfriend is the son of the German diplomat. His name is Cristos Breisacher."

Thor? The sound of my gasp filled the car's interior. *Claire! That psycho loon! I knew it! When I get ahold of her, I'm going strangle her with my bare hands.*

Sophie grasped my knee. "This entire situation is built on a tenuous house of cards, Holly, and the politics could become a nightmare for Gary, the FBI, everyone. We need to find out for sure. If it's true, we'll scramble the F-14s, the Marines, Coast Guard, Navy, whatever." She flapped her hand. "But we need more to go on. We need to confirm it's true."

"It is," I said with clarity. "Let's go get my babies." With renewed energy, I grabbed my coffee and hopped out of the car.

Everyone moved into overdrive. Sophie snatched up the bags of food, Ian and Ziggy opened the back lift gate and pulled out two black duffle bags. I didn't ask what was in them, and I'm pretty sure I didn't want to know. Ziggy led the way to a long, sleek, black and white Donzi power boat that had open seating for five. The name on the back read *Ashoka*.

"Whose boat is this?" I asked as I settled myself onto the back bench.

"You don't want to know," Ian said.

Sick of the secrecy, I snapped, "Of course I want to know, dammit! Whose boat is this?"

"Drug dealer." Sophie climbed in beside me.

It all clicked. Ziggy's reference in the car to the boat being "clean." I thought he meant washed down. He meant drug-free. Good to know if we got stopped during this escapade we wouldn't be arrested for drug smuggling.

"What does *Ashoka* mean?"

Sophie shrugged.

Ziggy was passing the duffle bags to Ian in the cuddy cabin, but he must have overheard my question. "*Ashoka* was an ancient Indian conqueror who killed all his brothers when his father died so he could become emperor. By the time he died, he ruled modern-day India, Pakistan, Nepal, and Afghanistan."

"Sounds like a charming man," I grumbled.

Ziggy's teeth flashed. "Eventually, he turned to Buddhism and is considered to have been one of India's greatest rulers."

Ziggy turned on the blower, pressed some of the shiny buttons on the dash, and revved up the engine. A few minutes later, the boat was running south, streaking along the California coastline like a high-end sports car. Sophie and I bundled close under a blanket, sunglasses on, our hair blowing behind us. Luckily, the nighttime winds had died down and the seas remained fairly calm. Once again, Ziggy drove and Ian rode shotgun. I realized they both wore all black, from the shoes to their leather jackets. It was all very *Miami Vice,* and if my girls hadn't been in mortal peril, I would have been able to appreciate the chance to ride in the racing boat. As it was, I was just glad Ziggy had associates who valued the need for speed.

Once we got south of Dana Point, Ziggy slowed and headed away from the coast, keeping an eye on the GPS. Catalina Island remained on our starboard bow with San Clemente Island further away portside. When we got abreast of Catalina, between the two islands, a red and white cruiser with Tow Boat US swathed across its bow passed about 500 yards off our starboard side. Ziggy circled around, hailed the driver, and pulled the Donzi up next to it.

A brief conversation told us what we needed to know. The mechanic had been able to fix the yacht, and as far as he knew, it was returning to shore, headed in our direction, back to the Dana Point marina. Neither the driver nor the mechanic had seen anyone else while they worked on the engine and electrical system and had no knowledge of who was aboard besides the captain who'd been hired to drive the vessel for the owner. He didn't think the craft was moving fast, and the Tow Boat driver figured we'd find it about five to six miles west of San Clemente. Ziggy thanked him and we roared away at such a pace, I figured I'd be picking gnats out of my teeth for the next week. I thought we'd been cruising fast before, but now the brawny engines pushed the long lines of the craft streaking across the waves. I pulled my coat tighter to keep out the wind.

Sophie thrust her phone in my face, and Gary's name blinked at me. She tapped Ziggy on the shoulder and showed him. When he saw the name, he powered down to an idle, but by the time the boat quieted the call had gone to voicemail.

"It's the second time he's called. I must have missed the first one," Sophie said.

Ian pulled his cell out of his pocket. "He rang me, too."

"Call him back," Ziggy commanded.

I shook my head. "I don't know what to say. And I don't like lying to him."

"You'd better ring him, luv. If he doesn't hear from you, he'll worry you're in trouble," Ian urged.

He was right. With burgeoning dread, I took Sophie's phone and dialed.

• • •

Gary must have been staring at the file for a good twenty minutes, grasping nothing as he flipped through the pages. He rubbed his eyes and checked the clock on the computer. His stomach rumbled, and he realized that he hadn't followed Holly's advice over an hour ago to get something to eat. Twenty minutes later he stood at the front of the busy bistro. Christmas music played over the speakers, and his eyes combed the patrons for a familiar face. He'd hoped they might still be here. Neither Sophie nor Ian had picked up their phones, and he was becoming increasingly frustrated that Holly didn't take her cell when she left the house. He scrolled the incoming call history and found a number for one of the agents stationed at the house.

"Agent Martin."

"This is Detective Sumner. Has Holly returned?"

"No, sir. She must still be out to breakfast with her sister."

"Okay. Thanks."

His phone rang and Sophie's number came up. "Sophie?"

"No, it's Holly. Sophie didn't hear her phone ring. What's up? Anything new?"

There was some sort of sound in the background that he couldn't identify. It sounded windy. *Was that a car engine?* "Where are you?"

"Still at the bistro. I told you we were getting something to eat."

His hackles rose and his cop instincts went on high alert. "Where are you sitting?" he asked casually.

"Um, about halfway back … one of the center tables. Why? Where are you?"

"At the bistro."

"Sh-shit," her voice hissed.

"I repeat, where are you? What's that noise I hear?" His question met silence as he swept out the restaurant door to gain privacy. *Jesus, this day couldn't get any worse. First the kids and now Holly is missing.* His heart sped into overdrive and his forehead broke out into a cold sweat. "Holly, what's going on? Are you okay?"

"Yes, I'm fine. Nothing is wrong."

"Are you on speakerphone?"

"No."

"Okay, if you're being held against your will, say 'the coffee is too hot.'"

"Gary, I'm not being held against my will. The coffee is fine. I'm with Sophie, Ian, and Ziggy. Guys, say hi."

She must have held up the phone because he heard a blend of voices.

Holly's voice came back. "Listen, I don't want to lie to you, but I can't tell you where I am."

"Why the hell not? What's going on?" He ran a frustrated hand through his hair, making it stand on end.

Shallow breaths came at him as he waited for an explanation, but the line remained silent.

"Holly," his voice softened, "tell me what is going on. You're scaring me, and frankly, I'm not sure I can stand losing another person today."

"I can't. I can't," her voice cracked. "You talk to him."

It sounded like the phone was fumbled around, and Gary heard intelligible conversation.

"Gary, it's Sophie. Holly is fine. Ziggy has a lead we're chasing."

"I believe Ziggy was told to coordinate with law enforcement if he came up with something."

"Yes-s, well, it's complicated."

"Then uncomplicate it for me," he gritted out.

"Uh."

"Sophie, you and I have been through a lot."

"Yes, I know."

"I think you owe me the courtesy of an explanation."

"Well, I can see how you would think that … but … we're in a situation where it would be best if you didn't know what we were doing."

Gary pressed two fingers against a temple. "Please tell me you're not breaking the law."

"We have not broken any laws …"

"Yet," he added for her.

She remained silent.

"Will Holly be safe?"

"Yes, of course. I wouldn't risk my sister's safety. It's better this way. Trust me. We'll be in touch soon. Very soon. If this works out, we'll have good news. If not, then we're not wasting law enforcement's time and taxpayer money."

"When it comes to my girls, I don't give a damn how much taxpayer money is used to find them."

"I get that. But, you're still a cop. And we … Holly … doesn't want you to cross any lines that can't be uncrossed."

"Your explanations are not reassuring."

"Gary, I promise you, we are doing what is best for you, Holly and the girls."

"Jesus," he hissed and worked to get a grip. "Please remind Ziggy that his private investigator's license has limitations. Additionally, remind your fiancé that he isn't really a cop, he just plays one on TV."

Sophie's laughter tinkled across the lines. "That's exactly what Holly said. Oh my, you two really are perfect for each other."

"Sophie," he ground out.

"Trust me. Now, time is of the essence and we really must go."

"Wait. Put Holly back on."

The phone was fumbled again and Holly's breathy voice came over the line. "Gary?"

"Please. Be safe."

"I will. Don't worry."

"That's a physical impossibility right now."

He heard a sob and Sophie's voice came back on the line. "Gary, breathe. Eat something. And take some time to rest. I promise we'll call soon. Bye." She hung up.

Next, he dialed the precinct.

"Suggs."

"It's Sumner."

"Gary, still nothing on your ex-wife's phone. The battery might be dead. We can't get it turned on remotely. The last call she made on it was two days ago, in a neighborhood in Lakewood. The area was thin of traffic cams, and what we do have has turned up nothing so far."

"You're still tracing my cell, right?"

"Yes, sir."

"Get me coordinates on the number that just called." He reeled off Sophie's phone number. "Get me an E911 ping on this cell number, too. Put a rush on it." He rattled off Ian's number. This shit was going to stop right now. Gary would be damned if he played a passive role while finding his daughter, and when he found those four he'd string them up by their big toes.

Chapter Fourteen

Ian held up a pair of binoculars and searched the seas until he pointed at something on the horizon. The cigarette boat adjusted its course, and the shape of a fifty-foot yacht expanded as we drew within a mile of it.

Ziggy powered down to an idle and turned back to us. "Either one of you know how to drive one of these?"

I shrugged helplessly and looked a Sophie.

"I've driven Adam's boat a few times. It's more of a fishing boat, nothing like this." She swished her hand, indicating the throbbing engines.

"Same idea. Come on up here."

Ziggy moved out of the way and allowed Sophie into the driver's seat. "She's got a lot more power than a fishing boat, and she planes out quicker, but the concept is basically the same. Once we get close, slow down and try to pull her up to the rear of the yacht. Ian and I will work the boat hooks so we can board quickly."

"Are you planning to board without permission? I don't want to cause some sort of international incident. Shouldn't we try to talk to them first?" Sophie cautioned.

"We lose the element of surprise if we hail them for a chitchat."

Sophie opened her mouth to speak, but I cut her off. "Screw diplomacy. I want my girls back. Besides, sometimes it's easier to ask for forgiveness than permission."

Ziggy's teeth flashed. "Let's suit up then."

Ian heaved one of the duffle bags on the passenger seat and drew open the zipper. Inside lay three handguns, one I identified as a Beretta, and some sort of assault rifles.

Ian hefted one of the rifles in his hand like it weighed nothing. "MAC-10 … lovely, where'd you get this?" He expertly drew back the slide and checked the chamber.

Ziggy rolled his eyes and shook his head, reaching for one of the handguns. "You don't want to know."

Suddenly, this caper became very real. Visions of Hollywood-style shootouts with stray bullets whizzing over the girls' heads came to mind, and I rethought Sophie's diplomacy angle.

"Hold up. Wait, wait." I put my hand on Ziggy's forearm. "Two little girls may be on that boat, and this isn't a movie, it's real life. We can't go in guns a-blazing. Someone will get hurt. Ian, put that down, please. Let's just … think about this. Even though I appreciate your … uh, preparedness, there's got to be some way to make this happen without Berettas and … and … that …." I flapped my hand at the assault weapon.

"MAC-10," Ian supplied.

"Right. MAC-10." You would have thought being married to a head of security for a Vegas casino and as a close friend with a cop, I would know more about guns, but I'd always found them a bit repulsive. A necessary evil you could say.

"I agree," Sophie backed me up. "There's got to be a better way. After all, we have no idea if anyone on the boat is armed. If we arrive aggressively, tensions will get jacked up and possibly put the girls in more danger."

Ziggy peered at me. "What do you suggest?"

"Uh …" I had no idea. I just knew that guns were dangerous and increased hostilities, creating a higher likelihood bullets would start flying. "Let me think a minute."

"All right, I've got it." Sophie snapped her fingers. "They don't know we are coming. So we have the element of surprise on our side. Moreover, Claire's never met Ziggy and Ian, so one of you boys should drive. Let's come in slow and hail their boat. Pretend we've got something wrong with ours. Once we pull aside, we can wrangle an invitation onto the boat. Holly, pull your hoodie up and tuck your hair into it. Ian, give me your hat. See? Holly and I will remain in the back and they won't know who we are until it's too late. Now boys, each of you take a fully loaded handgun and stick it in your back, so your coats cover them up."

I watched in awe as my sister masterminded the plan. The boys loaded clips into the handguns, checked the safeties, and jammed them down the back of their pants. Ian was a natural with the weapon. I knew he'd been trained for the show, but his comfort level impressed me.

"Do you want one, Sophie?" Ian asked.

She shook her head. "Leave the rest of the … hardware in the bag and put it on the floor. Close it up, but leave it unzipped …" *Just in case.* She didn't actually say the words, but we were all thinking them.

We trolled up to the yacht; Ziggy jerked his arm and *Ashoka* stalled out, almost directly in the path of the yacht. Ian blew an air horn we'd found in the glove box and hailed them. From the top we could see the captain wave at us and the vessel slowly drew alongside.

Ian had the boat hook at the ready, and Sophie tossed a fender over the side. The *Ulysses* drifted past, and in the rear stood a blond head that I recognized as Claire's boyfriend. Foolishly, I removed my sunglasses and our eyes met. Instant recognition flared. The jig was up.

Before I could warn the boys, Thor smiled and waved at us. "Ah, you are the mutter. No? It is good you came. The girls vill be happy," he said with a European accent.

Sophie and I exchanged confused looks while Ian threw a line to the smiling Nordic god. He caught it easily, and, with the help of the boat hook, the *Ashoka* pulled close to the rear and tied off. The fenders squishing and rubbing could be heard as the boats bobbed against one another. I pushed past my sister and stepped up on the back seat to navigate the height difference. Thor held out his hand and helped me clamber onboard. Sophie and Ian followed, while Ziggy remained behind. The blond man seemed nothing but cordial; however, I was glad to know that Ian had a gun tucked in his pants as our host drew back a darkened sliding door and I tensed, ready for possible violence. He led us into a luxurious living area, and it took a moment for my eyes to adjust to the altered light.

"Mommy!"

My knees sank to the ground, and my diminutive bundle of energy threw herself into my outstretched arms. The tension in my shoulders eased and the icy numbness that'd built around my heart over the grueling hours shattered. I held her tightly, burying my head into her soft locks. "Oh, my sweet pea." I sighed as tears flowed down my cheeks.

Eventually, she pulled away.

"Why are you crying? Are you hurt, Mommy?"

"No, baby, just something in my eye." I wiped the tears and searched for any sort of injury or hurt. She wore a purple princess costume and tiara that I'd never seen before. Pink-socked feet were jammed into plastic dress-up clogs. "Are you okay?"

"Yes, Mommy. The boat broke. It rocked a lot and Annie got sick. But I didn't. Annie's mommy said you'd come." She smiled. "I got to play the Wii. Want to see? Can we get one, Mommy?" She chattered at me, completely unaware how the past eighteen hours had affected the rest of us.

I hugged her tightly again. "Sure, pumpkin. I'll get you one for Christmas." I was so relieved that she was safe, I would have bought her a horse if she'd asked for it. "Where's Annie?"

"Down below."

I rose to face the watching audience. Sophie stood closest, with Thor behind her, and Ian just to his left, a little behind and clearly alert for any sort of hostility.

"Eva, stay here with your Aunt Sophie. Okay? Why don't you show her your dance moves?" My gaze shot to our host. "Take me to Annie."

With a Gallic shrug, he turned. "This vay."

To my relief, Ian followed the two of us down a narrow flight of stairs and along a short corridor, stopping in front of a brown wooden door. He pushed it open and stepped aside. My nostrils flared at the bitter smell of sickness.

A tiny lump lay curled up in the center of a large, circular bed.

"Annie?" I knelt beside the bed and pulled the covers back. Her hair was matted and dirty. She wore an oversized white T-shirt. "Pumpkin, it's Miss Holly."

She rolled over and opened her eyes. They were sunken, and dark circles ringed the lower lids. Recognition sparked and her lip trembled.

"I was sick," she croaked. A tear escaped the corner and tracked down the side of her nose.

"I know. I'm so sorry." I pulled her close.

Her arms weakly came around my neck. "Is Daddy here?"

"No, but I'm here to take you to him."

"Okay." She sniffed.

Ian stood in the doorway; there was no sign of Cristos. "Ian, can you see if they have some ginger ale? I'm afraid she's dehydrated."

I scooped Annie into my arms, carried her into the tiny bathroom, and sat her down on the toilet seat. I noticed there were remnants of vomit on the T-shirt she wore and a pink princess costume hung dripping over the shower door. "Let's get you cleaned up a bit and you'll feel better. Okay?"

Annie didn't say anything, just lay limp against the wall while I went back into the bedroom to rummage through the built-in drawers. On the floor lay a pair of plastic pink mules that matched Eva's. A quick whiff let me know that Annie must have been wearing them when she got sick. I found a petite ladies sweatshirt, and a quick search through a Cinderella backpack revealed the pair of jeans Annie had worn yesterday at the park. I laid the clothes on the bed and was about to return to the bathroom when a knock at the door interrupted me. Ian handed me a can of Canada Dry ginger ale and a straw.

"Do you need anything else?"

"See if you can find another backpack like this with Eva's stuff in it, as well as the girls' coats. And send Sophie down here. I may need her help."

With a nod, Ian disappeared and I returned to the bathroom.

"Here, Annie, I've got some ginger ale to settle your tummy."

"Daddy doesn't let me have soda. He says they're bad for me."

"I know, but this is a special soda for when you're sick. I don't think he'd mind."

After a bit more cajoling, I convinced Annie to take some sips, and then I set to work washing her hair in the sink and giving her a quick sponge bath. The soda and warm water seemed to perk her up a tad, and a few minutes later, Sophie arrived as I helped Annie pull on her jeans.

"Eva got her stuff and I found the coats." She stepped into the room and flinched, crunching her nose. "How's Annie doing?"

"Oh, I think we're going to be okay." I smiled at the little girl as we drew the sweatshirt over her head. It came to her knees and the sleeves hung well past her hands, dwarfing her. "This will keep you lovely and warm. Here, let me just roll up the sleeves."

"Can I have some more soda, Miss Holly?"

"Yes, of course." I handed her the can. "Remember, slow sips. You don't want to get sick again."

She nodded and sat on the bed with her drink.

"Has anyone seen Claire?" I asked.

Sophie shook her head.

"Stay here for a minute; I'll be right back." My gaze took in the short hallway. There were two doors, and I was trying to decide which one to choose when the door to my left jiggled and opened.

Claire stood for a beat in her silk dressing gown with a pink turban around her head, staring at me. I could almost hear the wheels clicking in her head.

A big smile flashed. "I'm so glad you're here. What an awful time of it poor Annie has had. We meant to get the girls back last night, of course. But the stupid engine broke down, and with the wind, we were blown so far off course." She shook her head. "Poor thing. I wasn't well myself. And Cristos was such a doll, running back and forth between the two of us. Oh" —she put a perfectly manicured hand against her breast—"I don't know what I would've done without my darling."

My brain exploded with fury, and I was on her so quickly she had no time to react. Reaching back with all my might, I let my hand fly. It met with a satisfying and resounding smack.

Screeching, she fell to the floor.

Damn, that hurt. How on earth did Omar slap me around without messing up his own hands? That woman must have had a jaw made of brick. I pivoted on my heel and found Sophie's head peeking at me from around the door to Annie's room.

"Did Annie see?" I whispered.

She shook her head. "Feel better?"

I rubbed my stinging fingers. As a victim of abuse, I usually found violence abhorrent. However, decking Claire seemed to foster no regrets. "Actually, yes."

Cristos bounced down the stairs and took in our tableau. His eyes dropped and rested on Claire. "Leibling, was ist los?" *What's going on?*

He hustled past me to get to her side.

Ignoring her bleating, I swept past Sophie, scooped Annie into my arms, and carried her weak little body to the upper deck. Eva stood next to Ian, her hand tucked trustingly into his, with her coat and a new Barbie backpack strapped on.

"Sophie, get Annie's coat on and the girls onto the *Ashoka* for me." She opened her mouth to speak, but I cut her off. "Please."

I started to pull Annie's arms away, but she gripped me tighter. "What's wrong, pumpkin?" I stroked her damp hair.

"Is Daddy going to put my mom in jail?" Her wide eyes revealed knowledge beyond her age.

"Why would you say that?"

"I heard her tell Cristos. When the boat broke and we couldn't get back on time, she cried and said Daddy would put her in jail."

I bit my lip as my mind warred with indecision.

"Don't let him put her in jail. Please, Miss Holly. Mommy just wanted to take us for a boat ride. We were supposed to be home at eight. It wasn't her fault. Please, Miss Holly, tell him it was an accident," she pleaded her mother's case to me.

What Claire had done was vastly illegal, and I desperately wanted to lock her up and throw away the key for the hell she'd put all of us through. Yet as her daughter begged me to save her from Gary's wrath and the justice system, I wavered.

"Please," she murmured, and her dark eyes shined bright with tears.

I pulled her tight. "I'll talk to them and see what I can do. Now, I want you to go with Eva and Sophie. Okay?"

She nodded and transferred easily into Sophie's arms. Crouching down, I pulled Eva's coat closed and zipped it up. "Eva, go with Aunt Sophie and Annie. Mr. Ziggy's outside in a big boat that will get us back to shore fast. Uncle Ian and I will be out in a few minutes."

Ian helped Sophie get Annie's coat on, and the three of them exited through the sliding door at the aft of the ship.

"What are you thinking, luv?" Ian crossed his arms and pierced me with his ice-blue gaze.

"Eva's growing up with a father in jail. As much as it pains me … I don't want Annie to have to experience the same stigma," I said grimly.

"Gary's not going to like it."

"I know."

"Hell." Ian scratched at his five o'clock shadow. "Who knows what the laws are surrounding a diplomat's ship? It's not like we're cops and have the authority to detain them."

"Good point. Can you go down and fetch Claire and Cristos?"

"You got it."

Restlessly, I paced the living room, picking up and subsequently putting down knick-knacks and straightening the couch pillows. A purple coat lay on the floor and, shaking it out, I laid it on a chair. As I fingered it, a snatch of conversation rose to my conscious, *A purple alien with a pink hat.* One of the children had seen what happened, but the adults hadn't understood the language and had ignored a vital piece of information.

The yacht gently rocked on the waves, and I shifted my weight to compensate for the movements. I found a piece of paper in a side table drawer and was jotting something down when the sound of footsteps met my ears. Claire, dressed in slacks and a sweater and holding an icepack against the side of her face, was helped into the room by Cristos. Ian remained in the doorway, I guess in case someone decided to run. Run where, I didn't know.

"Sit down." I indicated the couch.

Claire lowered herself down, as though she were a feeble octogenarian. Her frightened eyes darted warily back and forth between Ian and me while Cristos, on the other hand, gave me an angry glare, his bushy blond eyebrows in a V formation. His fearless irritation didn't surprise me, I'd walloped his precious *liebling* pretty well. My hand still smarted from the hit. Additionally, Cristos knew he had diplomatic immunity, whereas Claire, an American citizen, realized she would be prosecuted to the fullest extent of the law.

"You should not have hit her," Cristos ground out.

"Is the engine fixed?" I asked.

"Ja."

"Do you have enough gas to get down to Mexico?"

"Ja." His brows rose in puzzlement.

"Gentlemen, leave us, please."

Cristos looked as though he would deny my demand.

"Don't worry, I won't touch your girlfriend again."

Claire whispered something in a foreign language and seemed to be urging him to go. Finally, he rose.

Ian leveled his gaze at me, and those piercing blue eyes questioned my request.

I gave a nod. "It'll be okay." The door closed behind me, but my attention had already reverted to the matter at hand. "Claire," I barked.

She jerked and her face swung to mine.

"What was your plan with the girls? And don't you dare lie to me." I crossed my arms and glared at her.

"W-we were t-taking them on a s-sunset cruise?"

"Were you planning to take Annie away from her father?"

Her head shook vehemently back and forth. "No, no! You have it all wrong. Cristos has a new job to become diplomatic attaché … in Spain. I … I wanted to see Annie again before we left. I thought she'd like a ride on the *Ulysses*."

"Why'd you take Eva?"

"S-she wanted to c-come with us." Her eyes darted away from mine. "It was easier to take her. And besides, it was just supposed to be a few hours." She picked at some invisible lint on her trousers. "Cristos thought he could fix the problem, at first. But then the wind picked up, and we drifted … and we had to call the mechanic. Cristos wanted me to call one of you, but it got so late, then … I … I was afraid …" She gulped.

I stared up at the ceiling, grinding my teeth, and counted backward from ten before speaking again. "What about the custody hearing?"

Her shoulders moved up and down. "I was going to cancel it. Cristos can't really have children around right now. What with his career and now moving to Spain … and … Annie's not his child … and we're not married … yet. Well, that's why I wanted to see her, before I had to leave."

My hands balled into tight fists and I swung away, pacing in a tight circle. *God, the nerve of this woman!* "How did you plan to return the girls without getting caught?"

Her lips mashed together. "There's a trampoline park near Long Beach …"

I made a physical effort not to give her my squinty-eyed, paint-stripping stare, but I must not have done a very good job, because she winced and stopped speaking.

"Umm hmm, go on …"

"I-I was going to s-sign them up for jump t-time and call you to c-come pick them up."

"You. Were. Just. Going. To. Leave. Them?" I snarled.

"No! I would've waited in the car to make sure someone came … of course." She ducked her head in shame.

I sucked wind and counted again, this time starting at fifty. *The crazy train pulled into the station with Claire as the head engineer.* We needed to stop speaking about this, because her asinine plans were about to put me over the edge. My mind circled the options, and throttling Claire was starting to sound like an ideal plan.

By the time I'd counted to twenty, along with some yoga breathing exercises, rational thinking returned. I didn't know how complicit Cristos was in all of this, or if Claire had lied to him about the girls, but I'm pretty sure he knew that having them overnight was not part of the plan. Moreover, he'd put up no fuss when we arrived. He actually seemed relieved to see me and offload them. Closing my eyes, I pictured Annie's pathetic face begging me not to lock up her Mommy. Right now, I just wanted Claire and her boy-toy out of our lives. For good.

And I had a pretty fair idea how to make that happen.

Claire rocked back and forth, silently picking at a hangnail. I sighed and strengthened my resolve. "Listen up. You will tell your boyfriend to have the captain power up and head south, as quick as you can. Do not dock until you hit Mexico. Understand?"

Realization dawned in her eyes.

"If you set foot on American soil, I will not be able to, nor will I attempt to, stop Gary from arresting you and throwing away the key."

She nodded.

"I am giving you a gift today. In return for this gift, you will stay out of Annie's life." My hand slashed through the air. "You will dismiss the custody case."

Again, she nodded.

"But, as I am not a total monster and I love Annie, I will give *her* a chance … a chance to make her own decision in the future."

Claire gave me a confused look.

"You will set up a Yahoo account under this alias." I handed her the piece of paper. "When she turns eighteen, I will reveal this email account to her. She will choose if she wishes to contact you. You will not, I repeat, *will not*, come looking for her or make any attempt to contact her."

"Yes." She gulped and nodded.

"There will be no more custody hearings. Ever. Am I clear? This is nonnegotiable."

More nodding. "Why?" she whispered. "Why are you doing this?"

"Claire, you are the most compulsive, self-centered, narcissistic woman I've ever had the displeasure of meeting. You have your head so far up your own ass, you can probably see your uvula. However, you are not abusive, nor do I see deliberate unkindness from you. You are thoughtless and have caused pain and heartache. Luckily, no one has been physically hurt, and my own daughter, through her innocent eyes, sees this exploit as nothing more than a grand adventure. I'm not sure I can say as much for Annie, but she is young and still loves you. Because my daughter is growing up with the stigma of having her father in jail, and because Annie asked me, I won't do the same to her."

"Thank you." She fell to her knees and clasped her hands to her chest in a prayer position. "Thank you so much."

"I cannot speak for Gary. I will do what I can to keep him from coming after you." As I said this, I knew my actions would hurt and anger Gary so much, he might never forgive me. "That is the best I can do."

"I understand. Oh, thank you. Thank you. You are the kindest person I have ever, ever met. And Gary is a lucky man to have found you." She crawled forward on her knees, grasped my hand, and held it to her uninjured cheek.

My lips curled in disgust and I pulled it loose. "Get up and say good-bye to your daughter." With that, I strode out of the lavish living space. Cristos was nowhere to be seen, but the girls were aboard the *Ashoka* with Ziggy and Sophie. Ian remained on the *Ulysses*, holding the Donzi's rope close, ready to make a quick escape.

The big yacht's engines rumbled to life as I clambered aboard the idling *Ashoka*. Sophie had snuggled the two girls together under a blanket in the middle back seat and Ziggy entertained them by pulling quarters from behind Annie's ear. Her giggling laughter was a balm to my battered senses.

"Annie, say good-bye to your mom," I said in a cheerful voice.

Claire had put on a pair of sunglasses and followed me to the back of the yacht. "Good-bye, my darling. Mommy and Cristos have to leave because of his new job I told you about. You be a good girl for your daddy." She waved and blew a kiss.

Annie stood up and waved. "Bye, Mommy. Maybe we can visit you," she said naïvely.

Claire put a hand to her lips to hold back strong emotions. Her head bounced up and down and she waved maniacally. "Love you," her voice cracked.

By this time Ian had gathered the lines and boarded. The boats drifted apart slowly at first, and then Ziggy powered up, the *Ashoka* pulled away, and I breathed a sigh of relief. The girls were healthy and safe. God had answered my prayers.

Claire's parting sentiment didn't surprise me. I believed in her own way she did love Annie. Unfortunately, her mental issues made it impossible for that love to ever be enough. The niggling doubt of whether I made the right choice to let her go would probably always haunt me. Well, at least until Annie was eighteen. Until then, I vowed to God then and there as the sun shone down, and we sped along in our drug-running cigarette boat bouncing across the ocean waves, that I would love Annie like she was my own. I would do everything in my power to make sure she would never know a day without the proper love and care of a mother. I hoped Gary's anger would allow me to follow through on my pledge.

Chapter Fifteen

The Long Beach police launch bounced through the waves at a fast lick as Gary tightened the fastenings on his bulletproof vest. The wind whistled around his glasses as he balanced in the open prow of the boat, his service weapon, cuffs, mace, and an extra clip secured to his waist. All had been checked and rechecked to make sure they were in working order. He'd been browbeating the tech guys for the past hour. When the information finally came through, he could have kicked himself. Holly had been right to question Claire's whereabouts, and clearly Ziggy had gotten a bead on her. As his eyes searched the horizon, Gary mentally flogged himself for ignoring her instincts and suspicions about Claire.

He felt the telltale buzz of the phone against his thigh and pulled it out of the pants pocket. An unknown phone number blinked at him, and he ducked out of the wind under the center console overhand where the police sergeant skillfully drove the boat.

"Sumner." The engines and the airstream made it impossible to hear anything. He pressed the phone closer and put a finger in his other ear. "What? Hang on, I can't hear you." The person spoke louder, but again, nothing. He could only identify the voice as female. "*What?*"

"*It's Holly.*"

"Holly? Wait a minute." He tapped Sergeant Timmons on the shoulder and indicated he slow down.

The officer responded immediately.

"Where are you?"

"We're heading back to Long Beach." Her next words were music to his ears. "I have the girls."

His hand gripped the phone so tight he felt every curve and indentation. "Are they okay?"

"Yes. We're headed back to the Shoreline Marina in Long Beach. Meet us there with an EMT."

"An EMT?"

"It's just a precaution. Annie has been sick, and I think she's dehydrated. She was able to drink a can of soda, but it would be best if a professional checked her out."

Relief flooded his system, bringing tears to his eyes. He pressed his thumb and forefinger against the sockets to keep them at bay.

"Gary? Did you hear me? Annie is okay. She's going to be just fine. I promise."

He sucked the salt air through his nose. "I heard. Where's Claire?"

The phone remained silent for a moment as Holly digested his question. "So you know."

"I had a fair idea when I traced your location in the middle of the ocean between the California coast and San Clemente."

"How …?"

"Technology. Where are you now? Do you have Claire?"

"We do not. We just rounded San Clemente Island and are heading northeast toward Long Beach."

"Are you on Adam's boat? Tell me your location." A few months ago, Adam had taken Gary, Ian, and some guys from his office out on his Boston Whaler for a day of fishing and beer drinking. He was such an easygoing guy, it wouldn't surprise Gary if he'd lent his beloved boat for this escapade. "We're headed in your direction."

"Wait. You're on the water?"

"On a police launch."

"Oh."

"Right next to the depth finder you'll see the GPS—read me the coordinates."

"Uh, we're not on Adam's boat."

"Whose boat are you on?"

"… a friend of Ziggy's …" Her voice petered out and he heard her whisper, "He wants to know where we are."

"What kind of boat?" Gary asked.

"Donzi … black and white … like the kind from *Miami Vice*."

"Where the hell did Ziggy get a boat like that?"

"I'm not sure I'm at liberty to disclose that."

"What?"

"It's complicated."

"It's a boat. Someone owns it. It's not that complicated," he argued.

" … wait a minute. Hey, pumpkin. Did you have a good sleep? Do you feel better?"

"Holly?" Gary asked. She didn't answer him, clearly focused on one of the girls.

" … I'm talking to your daddy. You want to say hello?"

"Hi, Daddy." Annie's beloved voice crossed the phone lines and clamped onto his heart.

Gary softened his tone. "How are you, princess? Feeling better?"

"Yes, I was sick."

"I'm sorry to hear that. Holly's bringing you home and I'll be seeing you real soon."

"Okay."

As simple as that. If only his world could be as simple as his child's. "I love you, princess. Can you give the phone back to Holly now?"

"Love you, Daddy."

"Hello," Holly came back on.

"Give me the damn coordinates," he barked.

"I don't know where they are," she said in a singsong voice, clearly trying to maintain her cool in front of the girls.

This conversation that was going nowhere.

"I assume Ziggy masterminded this rescue and is driving."

"Well … actually, now that everything is okay, Ian wanted to take this baby for a spin. So he's at the helm now."

Gary ran a hand down his face and grunted. "Just … give the phone to Ziggy."

"Detective," Ziggy's deep voice crackled across the cell phone lines.

"Give me your GPS coordinates."

"Sorry, Detective, the GPS seems to be broken."

"Don't bullshit me. You're riding in a top-of-the-line racing boat. Where are you?"

"We'll get to Long Beach faster than you can catch up with us. Just meet us there." He ended the call.

The hell with that. Gary turned to the driver. "Get on the horn and get an EMT to Shoreline Marina in Long Beach. In the meantime, turn us west heading toward San Clemente Island."

"What are we looking for?"

"We're intercepting a Donzi, racing-style boat from what I can gather. Black and white."

"On it." The driver nodded and spun the wheel while accelerating at the same time. Gary grabbed hold of a rail as the boat heeled.

Twenty minutes later, one of the officers let out a shout and pointed. Two pairs of binoculars followed the direction of his finger. Sure enough, a black and white, low-slung boat whizzed along the waves. It was too far to make out the faces, but there were definitely two heads in front and an indeterminate amount of people in back. Gary signaled the sergeant to turn and give chase; as they came closer, the captain switched on the siren.

On the Donzi, heads turned, arms pointed, and the boat's wake dropped from a high rooster tail down to a trolling hump. The police boat approached from the rear, and as they got nearer, Gary's breath caught. On the rear seat stood his beautiful daughter, waving and smiling, Holly's arms banded around her waist. The police boat drew abreast of the rear platform, Gary leapt onto the slow moving Donzi, and, falling to his knees, he wrapped his arms around Annie.

• • •

With relief I released the death grip I'd had around Annie. Her impetuous act of hopping on the seat to wave at her father while Ian rapidly slowed the boat had scared me to death because she'd nearly fallen tips over tails off the back end. My heart dropped to my toes again as Gary hurdled from the moving police boat, over the water, onto the *Ashoka* in a jump worthy of a Hollywood action flick. I bent at the waist, hands on knees, and sucked wind in an effort to slow the rat-a-tatting in my breast.

"Welcome aboard, Detective," Ziggy drawled.

"Hiya, mate," Ian laughed. "Brilliant entrance. If you ever want a job as a stunt man, let me know."

Gary ignored both greetings, and like I had done not long ago, examined Annie for physical injuries, running his hands down her arms and back and searching her face for signs of discomfort. "You're really okay, princess?"

"I'm fine, Daddy. Miss Holly said you were meeting us at the dock."

"Well, I decided to come out and meet you instead."

She nodded at the simple answer. "Eva's down under with Miss Sophie; they were cold. But Miss Holly thought it would be better for me to stay outside so I wouldn't get sick again."

"A very good idea, indeed."

By this time, both the boats had stopped and the police launch bobbed next to *Ashoka*. One of the officers wearing full SWAT gear warily climbed aboard with an un-holstered weapon at his side.

"Whoa, officer. I don't think that will be necessary." Ziggy held up his palms.

Gary turned and jerked his head at the cop. "Not now," he grunted and the cop re-holstered the gun. I think the entire boat released a relieved sigh. After leaving the *Ulysses*, Sophie told me that the duffle bags, full of weapons with questionable origin, had been stowed away out of sight. I didn't ask but inferred they were hidden in the same compartments that usually housed the drugs. However, I noticed as he was driving that Ziggy still had the Beretta shoved down his pants. Out of the corner of my eye, I saw him nonchalantly pull his coat farther down his backside.

"We got to go on Cristos's boat with Mommy. But it broke and I was sick," Annie said to her father.

"Were you scared?"

The little girl looked down at her feet. "When I got sick and you weren't there. I cried for you."

"I missed you, too, princess." He hugged Annie again. "I'm glad you're back."

"Can we go home now?"

"Yup, jump up here and I'll help you onto the other boat."

Mentally, I breathed a sigh of relief, knowing we could put off the argument brewing between Gary and me for just a bit longer.

But Annie balked at this suggestion, pulling away with a shaking head. "Can't we ride home in this boat? With Miss Holly and Eva?"

I opened my mouth to encourage her to do what her father wanted, when her hand reached back and she tucked her cold fingers into my warm palm. The words halted in my throat. My own guilt and Gary's anger aside, Annie needed to surround herself with safety and people she knew. Almost everyone she trusted was on this boat, and I simply couldn't encourage her to get on another one with a bunch of strangers.

"Don't you want to go on the big police boat? We can turn on the siren if you want," Gary cajoled.

Annie gripped my hand tighter and stared with uncertain eyes.

"You're welcome to return with us, Detective," said Ziggy.

"Yes, Daddy. Let's stay. Please."

Gary hesitated, and the cop in him must have warred with the father, but Annie's pleas and her clinginess to me must have swayed him.

"Okay, princess."

"Yay." Annie clapped her hands, and Gary climbed over the back seat into the cockpit area.

He turned to the police officer still standing awkwardly on the back platform. "It looks like I'll be riding on this boat."

The officer nodded and climbed back over to the police boat.

"Hi, Mr. Gary." Eva waved from the cuddy steps.

"Hello, Eva. Did you get sick, too?"

Eva gave a cheeky grin. "Not me. I played Wii. Mommy says we can get one for Christmas." Her head disappeared back into the cabin.

I rolled my eyes.

"She seems to be doing okay," Gary said evenly.

"Yes. To Eva, last night was apparently an exciting adventure that included no specific bedtime, candy, and video games," I returned with a dispassionate voice.

I breathed a sigh of relief as Gary, still in cop mode, moved to the side of the boat to conference with his fellow officers on the police launch. Annie curled back into my arms, and I hummed quietly, enjoying the warmth her little body emitted, and stared off toward the horizon.

"Holly."

My attention snapped back to Gary.

"Where was the *Ulysses* headed?"

I knew the discussion needed to happen; however, I wasn't quite ready for it, and not in front of Annie. She seemed to be drifting on the edge of sleep and I hesitated to wake her, so I took the chicken way out and hid behind the child. I shrugged and hummed louder in hopes Annie wouldn't understand what the discussion was about. She'd made no movement when Gary mentioned the *Ulysses*, so I could only hope that the child didn't know the name of the boat her mother traveled aboard.

"Anyone notice which way they went?" Gary looked around at the other passengers. Ian's gaze remained facing forward; Ziggy watched the detective with a neutral look.

"Anyone?" His one brow rose high in disbelief.

"It was heading north, and the captain said something about San Francisco," Ziggy replied.

If I didn't know better, I would have sworn Ziggy spoke the truth.

Chapter Sixteen

My legs gave out and I flopped onto the couch cushions, relieved that the longest day of my life was coming to a happy end. Eva and Annie were safe. An EMT checked out both girls at the marina; Annie was given fluids and told to rest. Undoubtedly, she'd be right as rain within the next twenty-four hours.

I'd sidestepped Gary's questions the entire afternoon and stuck close to the girls as an excuse not to get into further discussions. I knew I'd need to make some sort of statement. Gary requested that all of us—Ian, Sophie, and Ziggy—come down to the precinct to give statements and tell our side of the story in the morning. However, there were private things I needed to say to him, and the questions that needed answering were better asked in private.

On the way home, Sophie informed me that Mom had arrived from Arizona and was anxiously awaiting my return. Apparently, once Poppy heard that the girls had been found safe, she escaped my mother's clutches and headed to work. I arrived home to find Mom chatting and basically making a nuisance of herself as the agents disassembled mission control, returning my dining room back to its main purpose.

I graciously thanked agents Roland and Martin for their help on the case, and they politely accepted my thanks, even though we both knew it had been Ziggy's investigative skills and questionable business contacts that'd ultimately found my little girl. After the feds left, I made a mental note to have Ziggy sweep for bugs.

Mom put Eva to bed, then came to find me slouched on the sofa.

"I can't believe how much she's grown since Halloween."

I nodded as she folded herself onto the club chair.

"You look wiped out. I can't imagine how you've held it together without falling to pieces." Her sturdy hands pulled a woven Indian blanket across her lap, and she pushed a lock of grayish-blond hair behind her ear. Shrewd, green eyes that I knew almost as well as my own studied me, searching for a chink in my armor.

I thought about how she'd dealt with the blow of my father's unexpected death and how strong she'd been during that horrible time. A year ago, when I'd fled Omar's clutches, she dropped everything and flew out even though I encouraged her not to come, and I was so comforted when she did. She'd been there for me and my sister as Sophie recovered from a bullet wound and I began rebuilding my life. Mom was always there for me, for us. Even though her gregarious personality could, at times, be overwhelming, she was kind and loving, and though I'd originally cringed when Sophie told me Dorothy Hartland would be arriving on my doorstep a few days early, right now, I was grateful to have her here.

"I must take after my mother." I grinned. Her face softened and the crow's feet deepened as she returned my grin.

"You know, Poppy gave me a fudgy story. Mind letting me in on the truth about what really happened?"

Briefly, I ran down the highlights, including my deal with Claire and ending with my subsequent lack of telling Gary exactly what happened on board the *Ulysses*. "Tomorrow I've got to make a statement at the police station, and I'm not sure what I'm going to say." I yawned.

Her wise eyes regarded me and her head slowly moved up and down. "You're hiding this from him, and it's eating away at you. Isn't it?"

I blinked and looked away from a probing gaze that knew me too well.

She patted my knee. "Go talk to him, or you'll never sleep tonight."

The nighttime temperatures had dropped into the thirties, and I stuffed my hands deeper into the coat pockets as I tramped down the sidewalk. I'd texted Gary, and as I strode up the brick path, the front door opened. His silhouette waited.

I found neither the caring friend nor the stone-faced cop mien I'd come to expect. Instead, a grim stranger stood in front of me. His facial hair had long surpassed the five o'clock shadow phase, and the rings below his eyes gave him a haggard look, even though his cheeks were red and chapped from the boat ride.

The Christmas tree lights burned bright, illuminating the living room, and I rotated in a circle, coat on, trying to figure out what to say and how to begin. Gary made no move to make it easy for me. He stood with arms crossed, and those hazel-brown eyes staring at me remained cold as a leaden winter sky.

I swallowed. "C-can I sit down?"

One of his hands indicated the sofa. I lowered myself and patted the cushion next to me.

He didn't move. Didn't bat an eyelash.

I drew in a breath. "Okay, then. I bet you're wondering why I came over."

"I suspect it has something to do with the rescue of our girls on a known drug runner's boat."

Okay, so he figured out the Ashoka belongs to drug runners. "If you know the owner is a drug runner, why hasn't he been arrested?"

"Not my department, but that's beside the point. What I'd like to know is how you and the girls came to be on it."

"You're right. You deserve an explanation." I fidgeted with my fingers.

"I deserve a more than a fucking explanation."

My gaze snapped up at that. Gary wasn't one to throw the f-word around, and I realized his anger barely simmered below the surface; a vein bulged at his temple and his jaw was locked as tight as a vise-grip.

"I deserve the truth, which you've been skirting all day, and my patience is wearing thin. Don't take me for a fool, Holly." Probably in consideration of his sleeping child, he spoke in a low but lethal volume, taking an absurd amount of strength to restrain himself when it was obvious he wanted to roar at me.

"Yes, you deserve the truth," I said, nodding, "but let's not forget where we found the girls and who they were with."

"I'm well aware who they were with, and I'm doing everything in my power to find her and bring her to justice."

I tried to hide my gasp and said in a small voice, "Stop, please."

"What? Stop what?"

"Call off the dogs. Let Claire go."

Dark brows V'd over his narrowed, steely glare, but I swallowed the dread creeping up my esophagus.

"Did you hit your head and lose your mind? Have you somehow forgotten what's happened in the past twenty-four hours? She put our children in danger and committed a felony. I can't just 'call off the dogs.' This is an open investigation until she and her partner in crime are found."

"You don't understand." I pressed cold fingers against the grinding pain at my temples. "It'll be better for everyone if you just let it go."

"What are you talking about? Better for whom?" He placed a dining room chair in front of me, flipping it backward and straddling it. The unreadable cop face replaced the harsh glare. "Is there something more to this rescue you aren't telling me?"

I shook my head and squeezed my eyes shut against the quick flash of pain that sliced through my retina. *I should have waited until morning. I shouldn't have allowed my mom to talk me into doing this now. I should have made a better plan.* Both my brain and body needed sleep to recharge, and I desperately wanted this conversation to be over.

"Is she dead? Did one of you kill her while rescuing the kids?"

My eyes flew open and I reared back with a hand to my chest. "God, no! Absolutely not. How could you think such a thing? Claire was fine when we left. Not a shot was fired. There was no violence. Well, except for …" I clamped my mouth shut.

"Except for …"

"… all right, I smacked her."

"You … smacked her."

"Hard. Totally bitch-slapped. She fell to the floor."

Gary sat back and the crossed arms returned. But now they were accompanied by a slight lift of his lips. "Why don't you tell me what happened on the *Ulysses*?"

"Let me clarify one thing. Ziggy suggested we keep you and the FBI in the dark for two reasons." I held up two fingers. "First, because the *Ulysses* belongs to a German diplomat. Second, his intelligence was … shifty."

His brows rose. "Shifty?"

"Dubious. From a dubious source."

"Could that source be the owner of the *Ashoka*?"

"Perhaps. But as I was saying, since the boat belonged to a diplomat, Ziggy had concerns that in order for law enforcement to board, they'd need to get permission from the State Department. It had the potential to become an international incident."

"That wasn't for Ziggy to decide."

"You're right. Ultimately, it was my decision. I take responsibility for withholding the information."

Gary's mouth worked and I waited for him to blast me. "Go on."

"Ziggy gained access to a fast boat."

"Wait … 'gained access.' Please tell me he didn't steal the drug runner's boat for this absurd rescue mission."

"No! The drug runner let Ziggy borrow it." I slapped a hand across my mouth while Gary pursed his lips, clearly pleased with his success at obtaining the very information I'd endeavored to hide from him.

"Don't stop. This conversation is quite revealing."

"You don't understand. Time was of the essence, and we felt there was a higher likelihood of success on our own, without trigger-happy police possibly causing some sort of shootout."

"So, you're telling me you approached a possibly armed crew without any weapons and no backup? Explain to me how on earth that was safe for any of you—the kids, Sophie, Ian?"

I ground my teeth to keep from blurting out that we hadn't gone in unarmed. I wasn't so sure all of Ziggy's weapons (a) had been acquired legally, or (b) were legally registered. MAC-10s didn't seem to be the type of weapon you shopped for at the local sporting goods store.

"It turned out there was no need for weapons. As soon as Cristos realized who I was, he welcomed me aboard and was quite happy to offload the girls. As a matter of fact, I have a feeling we have him to thank for taking care of Annie while she was ill. It seems your ex had her own difficulties with the fitful seas last night and went to bed with a headache," I said, dramatically lying across the couch and sweeping a hand to my forehead like a Victorian debutant in an effort to lighten the mood.

"Why didn't you stop them from leaving?"

My diversion didn't work, and with wide-eyed honesty I met his gaze. "I had no power to do so. None of us were law enforcement. The yacht belonged to a diplomat and ..." I shrugged.

"And?"

"Nothing. That's it." My eyes left his and darted around the room, to the tree, a hanging clock, my hands.

"Somehow, I have a feeling that Ziggy is crafty enough that if he wanted to disable Cristos's boat, he would have figured out some way to do so. His inactions tell me someone told him not to."

"That's a big supposition." I crossed my legs, refusing to meet his gaze.

"You're lying to me. I'm not quite sure what you're lying about. But I know you're lying to me."

I remained silent.

"Who are you covering for? Ziggy? Your sister? Ian?"

My head shook in denial.

He let out a gusty sigh and pushed to his feet. "Holly"—his feet paced the carpet while his fists clenched and unclenched— "I need to know what happened and you need to be the one to tell me. I'm sure I can break your sister, possibly Ian. Someone's going to tell me. If it's not you … I'm not sure where we stand."

My throat went arid, and I had to swallow twice to get the question out. "What do you mean?"

"How can I trust you if you won't tell me the truth?"

And here we were—at the crux of all my fears and concerns. I breathed deep in through my nose, out through my mouth to calm the acid roiling in my stomach. "Who is asking? My friend Gary, Annie's father, or the cop?"

"They're the same person."

"No, they're not. My good friend and Annie's father is willing to listen without condemnation and judgment. The intimidating cop considers all angles and determines a legal course of action." He paused his pacing as I speared him with my gaze. "So, whom am I speaking to right now?"

An emotion I couldn't pinpoint fluttered across his countenance. Without a word, he removed his badge and gun from his belt and placed them on the scarred coffee table. Then his jaw relaxed, his scowl fell away, and for the first time since before the kidnapping, his features softened. A moment later he lowered himself next to me on the sofa.

"The detective has left the building." He flashed a smirk that made my heart skip a beat. "It's just me, Gary. Your best friend and confidant. Now, please, tell me what happened."

"I'm afraid that even Gary, my friend, will be angry."

"Holly." His callused hand closed around mine. "I need to hear what happened, and even though there's a war going on within you, I can see that you need to tell me, too."

"Yes," I whispered, "but, I'm afraid what I'm going to tell you will be the end."

"Telling the truth will never be the end. But keeping it from me …" He shrugged.

He was right of course; I both longed and dreaded telling him. I tried to imagine having a life without Gary and Annie in it, but I couldn't. Quite simply, they were as much my family as Eva and Sophie. My vow on the boat came to mind; I knew I needed to confess, and I prayed my confession wouldn't drive him away. Fingers scrubbed at my gritty eyes, and I released an audible sigh.

"I made a deal with Claire."

Silence.

"She will stay out of Annie's life. No more attempts to gain custody or visitation. No more seeing Annie at all."

"And?"

"I wouldn't turn her over to the police. To you. I told her to run and never look back."

"Run where?"

I didn't speak, just shook my head.

Gary stiffened and his shoulders tensed. "That wasn't your call to make."

"You're right. It wasn't my call. It was Annie's," I whispered.

"What do you mean?"

"Annie begged me not to let you arrest her mommy. And … I didn't want your little girl growing up with the shame of having a convicted felon for a parent, the way my daughter will."

He deflated, sagging against the cushions, for once at a loss for words.

"I didn't want you to feel what it's like to put your ex, the mother of your child, in prison, knowing it would hang over your head the rest of your life. Claire's actions were foolish and irresponsible, but she never had any intention of hurting the girls."

He ran a hand through his already tousled hair. "Do you know where they were heading?"

I remained stone-faced, neither admitting nor denying his question.

"I take it that's a yes."

"Are you going to go after her?"

His gaze dropped to his feet. "I … don't … know."

I barely heard the whisper. "What does it matter where she goes as long as she never sets foot on U.S. soil again?"

"Was that part of the deal?"

"Yes."

"Do you believe she will honor the agreement?"

I mashed my lips together. *Were Claire's mental faculties well enough to know to stay away? Would Cristos keep her out of the States?* "If she doesn't, she knows she'll be pursued by the police and prosecuted … and I won't stand in the way."

"Is that all?"

I bit my lip. *Should I tell him about the e-mail account?* "That's all."

Abruptly, he stood. The pacing returned.

"Gary?"

"You had no right. No *right* to make that deal. I'm Annie's father. This was my call!" he declared, viciously stabbing a finger at me.

My hackles rose. "And *E-v-a,*" I pronounced each syllable with slow care, "is my daughter. *Mine.* She, too, was kidnapped by *your* ex-wife and found because one man listened to me and followed my instincts." I didn't add that he wasn't that man, but the unsaid words floated around us like a wraith whispering across the air.

His shoulders jerked as though I'd physically punched him. "I think you should leave," he ground out harshly.

Realizing that I'd pushed too far, I got to my feet and gulped back the lump that rose in my throat. "Gary, wait, I'm sorry. Please, don't be angry."

"I'm not angry." He stared at the shimmering tree.

"You are. You have a right to be. But don't let this drive a wedge between us. Don't push me away."

"You betrayed me."

There it was. My gut clenched and the air drove out of my lungs. Exactly what I feared would happen the moment I made the bargain with Claire and allowed that boat to head south to Mexico. I'd put Annie's needs above Gary's. I knew, better than anyone, that betrayal was a tough hurdle to leap. "I didn't mean to betray you. I … I just did what I thought was right."

"I should have found Claire first. *I* should have known she would do this."

"What? No. Don't blame yourself. How could you have known?" I cried. "Who knows their ex would do something like that? That woman's head is like a bag of cats."

"I know." He turned away, stuffing his hands in his pockets. "I dragged my feet finding her. Once we determined the kidnapper wasn't Holtzman, I figured it was some felon I'd put away. I didn't want this kidnapping and the dangers that my job places Annie in to be used as an excuse for Claire to gain custody."

He refused to search for Claire because of the custody case? This declaration was both disillusioning and unwelcome. However, his next statement didn't allow me to reflect further on the admission.

"But she's crossed the line this time. Crazy or not, I don't know if I can just 'let her go.' Deep down, I'm livid that you guys let her slip through your fingers. One way or another, she needs to pay."

"Letting Claire go was my fault. My decision. Don't blame the others. And believe me"— the image of Claire's crumbling face as we drove away flashed in my brain—"she's paying for her mistakes, and will continue to pay for years to come."

Gary speared me with a skeptical glower.

"No, listen to me; she'll feel the pain of losing her daughter every day. Even though she'll live her life, she knows … *knows* … her actions will never let her return to the country of her birth and her daughter who will grow up without her. She'll never watch Annie learn to read, celebrate after winning a soccer game, ride a bike, or attend her graduation. Never again will she get to hear Annie's laughter and joy. Maybe today she's congratulating herself on making a clean getaway. But, trust me, the anguish I saw in her eyes as she said good-bye will linger and return, again and again. She may fill her life with parties and playboys, but as the years pass, what she gave up will eat at her, and I imagine one of a few things will happen. She could return to be arrested in hopes that Annie will visit her in prison. However, considering her narcissistic tendencies and survivalist personality, it's more likely that what she's done will make her a regretful shell of a person. Always looking back as the future extends before her with a hole in her heart—absent her daughter's love." The latter not on I mumbled under my breath.

During my speech, Gary remained with his back to me staring at the tree, so I had no idea if my words sank in. The headache continued to throb behind my eyes, and the adrenaline or cortisol that had kept my body going over the past thirty-some hours drained from my system like a deflating balloon, leaving me weak and exhausted. It felt like I'd run a marathon, and suddenly, I had neither the energy nor the inclination to continue defending my actions.

As much as I desired Gary's forgiveness, even more I craved rest. My body and mind needed the soothing rejuvenation of sleep. Undoubtedly, Gary needed the same, and continuing this discussion would get us nowhere. At least nowhere we wanted to go. I'd done what I needed to do.

"I can't do this anymore. My mind is a misty muddle, and I can't think straight. Perhaps you're right; it's time I left." I hauled myself to the door and paused. "I can forgive your inaction … perhaps you can find it in your heart to forgive my actions." I turned the knob. "I'll see you at the precinct tomorrow. If you want to leave Annie with my mom, drop her off before you go. I've told Sanvi to take the rest of the week off."

The frigid air washed over me as I left Gary standing like a statue in front of his Christmas tree. My heart ached in a way I never thought possible. In the past day, I'd struggled with incredible strain and fear and tension, but nothing felt like this vise squeezing my heart. Once again I wondered if I'd done the right thing. *Will Gary forgive me? Will Eva and I have to learn to live without the Sumners and my pledge go unfulfilled?* Questions hammered my head as I dragged myself step by step home.

• • •

The click of the closing door met Gary's ears, its sound so final. For a moment he vacillated between following or letting her go. Not long after she'd gone, the anger abated and rational thoughts began to break through the ire. He'd beaten himself up all afternoon for not directing the search for Claire sooner, and now he blamed Holly for letting her go. But one thing she'd said rang true: Neither Holly nor her compatriots were law enforcement. Not one of them had the authority to hold up a diplomat's boat, much less force one of its occupants off it. Not even Ziggy. He had a feeling the boat, contrary to Ziggy's initial assertion, was headed south to Mexico. Whether or not Holly knew the truth of their direction was still unclear, and one of the things weighing on his heart.

Eventually, he tumbled into bed, but his dreams were splintered and littered with the fractured feeling that he continually chased someone who remained elusive and out of reach. Twice he woke with a start and checked on Annie to reaffirm that she was home, safe, in her bed.

What slowly became clear through the night as the red haze of anger and self-flagellation lifted was that Claire's antics had driven a canyon-sized gulf between Holly and him.

Then something he remembered hearing at a mandated therapy session following his first on-duty shooting came to mind: *I control my own actions and my response to others.*

That thought brought a clarity he'd been lacking since he first heard his daughter had gone missing; it was as though the draperies opened to reveal the truth.

I allowed my reaction to Claire's antics to drive us apart. Claire doesn't have the power to ruin my future happiness. Only I carry that power. Why am I allowing my past with her to cloud my future happiness with a woman as incredible as Holly?

Gary was on the front porch, closing the door behind him, before he realized that it was two in the morning and his daughter lay sleeping in her room. *Damn.* He couldn't leave. Instead he texted Holly.

Are you awake?

No response.
He texted again.

Holly?

After twenty minutes, he gave up on receiving a reply. *Where is my head? Of course she's not awake.* The poor girl looked as ragged as an American flag left out in a hurricane and was probably sleeping like the dead. Eventually, he fell into a dreamless sleep.

His ringing cell woke him. The sun streamed through the open blinds and the clock read eight thirty.

"Hello," he rasped.

"Did I wake you?" Holly asked.

"Yes, but I needed to get up anyway."

"I'm sorry, I just looked at your text this morning. Is everything okay?"

"Yeah, I'm glad it didn't wake you."

"Did you need something?"

He could hear Annie in her room, playing and singing quietly to herself. "No … did you get some sleep?"

"Yes, my body was so depleted I fell into bed and knocked right out." Her voice sounded guarded, not her usual sweet demeanor.

"Listen, I know I'm not really in a position to be asking favors, but I'd like to take you up on you offer last night. Can your mom watch Annie today while we go down to the police station?"

"Yes, of course. Would you prefer if Mom brought Eva over to your house? So Annie can stay in her own home?"

"That would be great."

"What time do we need to be at the station?"

"I told your sister—or I should say, your sister told me—she needed a rest and she'd be there at ten. Ian said he'd swing by after work this evening. Ziggy said he'd be there at ten with Sophie."

"I'll bring them over at nine thirty."

An hour later, he opened the door to Eva.

She bounced across the threshold and hugged his leg, "Hi, Mr. Gary. Where's Annie?"

His heart lurched at the action, and he grinned at her smiling face, relieved that this adorable little girl was none the worse for wear from her recent escapade. "In the kitchen, finishing breakfast."

"Guess what?" she hollered, skipping past him to join her friend. "Nana's taking us to see Santa!"

Annie answered with a resounding, "Yay, Santa!"

Mrs. Hartland, looking neat as a pin dressed in slacks and a sweater set, followed Eva and embraced Gary in a fierce hug. "Oh, my dear boy. What a terrible trial you've had. You poor thing. I don't know how you and Holly have held up. I would have been a useless watering pot through the entire ordeal." She patted his newly shaved cheek. "Don't you worry now, I'm here to take care of the little ones and no harm shall come to them under my watch. You can be sure of that." She bustled past him, un-shouldering an overflowing tote. "Girls, Nana brought you a Minnie Mouse puzzle."

The sounds of excited chattering followed her announcement, but Gary's eyes fastened onto Holly, who remained in the car watching as her mother and daughter entered. She gave a brief wave, shifted into gear, and pulled away from the curb.

Damn. His mea culpa would have to wait.

Chapter Seventeen

Sophie exited her CR-V as I entered the police station parking lot and pulled into the adjoining space.

"Hey, sis," she gave me a brief hug and squinted. "You look … 80 percent better. Did you get some sleep?"

"Slept like the dead. Where's Ziggy?"

"We came separately. I think that's his SUV over there. He must already be inside."

"Wait." I gripped her forearm.

"What's up?"

"I told Gary about my deal with Claire."

"When?"

"Last night."

Her gaze searched my face and her brows lowered with concern. "How did he take it?"

"Not well. He accused me of betraying him. Which is basically what I did."

"Ouch."

"Yeah, tell me about it."

"I wondered why you two didn't show up together this morning. Did you tell him about Mexico?"

"No, but I'm pretty sure he suspects something." I shook my head, staring down at my pink and gray plaid Chucks. "Since I awoke this morning, I've been questioning my actions. What I said, what she said keeps running through my head. Did I allow Annie's emotions to affect my better judgment? Maybe I should have detained Claire and let the police sort this out. Now it's a mess."

"Holly, stop." Sophie gripped my biceps and gave me a shake. "You've got to stop questioning yourself. First, how on earth were you going to detain her? Physically drag her off the boat? Tie her up and everyone else on the boat? I'm pretty sure Cristos and the captain would have had something to say about that. Cripes, I can't imagine the heap of trouble we'd have made if we'd used those guns to force them. That definitely would have started an international incident. Long and short, no one had the power or authority to stop that boat or to remove Claire from it."

"I *told* her to run to Mexico."

"So? So what? You didn't tell Gary. Hell, you didn't even tell me what exactly went on in that room between you two. Who's to know what you said? Besides, they are grown adults. You didn't hold a gun to her head and say 'go to Mexico.' Claire makes her own decisions. And from what I can tell, she's a professional at running away to save her own ass, illegal or not. I'm sure it would have occurred to them to dock somewhere beyond the U.S. borders. Gary's just going to have to see that."

"I don't know. There's not a lot of gray with Gary; he's very black and white at times."

"Well, our detective is just going to have to get over himself. Hmph." Her steady blue gaze held me as tightly as the fingers digging into my biceps.

"You're right, okay. Um … ouch, do you think you can loosen up a bit?"

"Oh, sorry." She released me and I rubbed my arms.

"Let's do this."

A uniformed officer escorted us back to the detectives' bullpen. Mild murmurs and the click of computer keys were punctuated by bursts of ringing phones; it was a relatively quiet morning. A maze of chest-high cubes separated the detectives' desks. To my left I spotted Ziggy being led by a detective I didn't recognize into a room that I recognized very well as interrogation room B. The small, dreary room housed two chairs and a metal table bolted to the floor. Unlike the cop shows on TV, there was no two-way mirror; instead, three cameras spread through the room, and the walls were covered in an ugly ochre, sound-dampening corkboard. This was not a room innocent people making statements visited.

"Why are they taking Ziggy into interrogation?" I questioned the uniform standing to my left.

"Routine, ma'am. I believe Detective Ramirez will be taking your statement. Let me just … Here he comes."

A black-haired Hispanic man of medium height in a black suit strode the walkway between cube-world toward us. I recognized him from the company picnic.

"Ramirez." I stepped around the uniform. "What's going on?"

"Thank you, Sergeant, I'll take it from here. Holly, why don't you and your sister follow me?"

He led us to a small conference room with a wooden table and six chairs. "Have a seat."

Sophie and I shed our jackets and arranged ourselves across from the detective. "What's happening with Ziggy, Ramirez?"

"The LAPD simply has some questions about his relationship with the owner of the boat you were on, and what he knew and when he knew it."

Sophie giggled. "You're kidding, right?"

Ramirez's long face showed clearly this was no joke.

Sophie's smile fell. "You're not joking?" she whispered.

"This is preposterous. Whom do I speak to about this?" I rose.

"Please, sit down."

"No, I will not sit down. It's the most outrageous thing I've heard. While you and the FBI sat around with your dicks in your hand, that man found and rescued my daughter and, need I remind you, the daughter of Detective Sumner."

Ramirez's face turned red during my little tirade, but he kept it together. "We're aware, Miss Hartland. I'm sure Mr. Zagarelli will be just fine. Now let's sit down and get your statements." The detective opened his laptop.

"No." I was at the door in a second.

"Miss Hartland, wait."

But there was no way I'd allow Ziggy to twist in the wind while the police stalled me. I'd watched enough *Law & Order* to recognize a placating tactic when I saw one. Across the room, Gary entered with his cell to his ear and a manila folder in the other.

"Gary Sumner," my imperious voice rang out.

He held up a finger.

I weaved my way through the narrow walkways at a fast clip, mumbling. "Oh, hell no. You do *not* just hold your finger up at me. I don't care what kind of bee you've got up your butt." Behind me I could hear Ramirez's footsteps following my path. Heads prairie-dogged up as we passed by.

By the time I reached Gary, he'd hung up. "What the hell is going on? Ziggy's in interrogation room B."

"I just heard." His eyes bypassed me, and he acknowledged his colleague with a tilt of his chin. "Ramirez."

Sophie stuck her head around Ramirez's left shoulder. "What's going on?"

"I'm not exactly sure. Wait with Ramirez while I go find out."

He turned away, but I wasn't to be deterred. I followed him into the technology room where the detectives could watch the interrogations. Three different monitors showed Ziggy and his interrogator from different angles. Ziggy reclined with his legs kicked out to the side, his girth dwarfing the little metal chair. Ramirez stood in the doorway; Sophie elbowed her way past him and stared open-mouthed at our friend.

"So, Mr. Zigarelli, you maintain that the drug dealer Carlos Suarez told you that he saw the boat leave the harbor." The detective leaned forward across the table as he questioned Ziggy.

"Alleged drug dealer." Ziggy responded.

The computer technician looked up from the monitors. "Hey, Detective."

"Who ordered this interrogation?" Gary asked.

"Dunno, but I heard the FBI was pissed they were outsmarted by some hack P.I. and gave the chief an earful."

"Is the chief at the precinct today?"

"I believe so," the tech replied.

Gary snatched up the desk phone handset, then punched in a combination of numbers. "Chief, this is Detective Sumner. I'm in interrogation. Is the DA charging Mr. Zigarelli? … I see … yes, perhaps that would be best." His mouth flattened into a straight line. "The chief will be joining us."

Ten minutes later, the overcrowded room was filled with cross-conversations, sharp voices, and my sister's incensed shrill. A detective by the name of Calvin had been pulled out of interrogation room B to join us, leaving Ziggy to twiddle his thumbs, looking unruffled and cool as a mint julep on Kentucky Derby race day. Calvin, along with Gary, the computer tech, the chief, an assistant district attorney, Sophie, and I, clustered together in the bread box-sized space, literally rubbing shoulders with each other. The crowded quarters were almost as unbearable as the tapestry of unintelligible legal jargon that wove around me, threatening my sanity.

"*Stop it! Stop it! Stop it!*" I pushed my hands against my ears to block out the harsh tones, elbowing the computer tech in the head as I did so.

The arguing shut off like a tap and all eyes swiveled to me.

"Holly—" Gary said.

"No! I hired that man" —I pointed to Ziggy on the monitor— "to find my daughter. Which he did! His methods may be unorthodox, but they got the job done. What you're doing is unprofessional. Eva and Annie were safely rescued due directly to this man's perseverance. He followed a lead, which no one in this department was willing to follow. This is a witch-hunt because he embarrassed both you and the FBI. Now you're looking to drum up charges against him because you're pissed. There were no drugs on the boat we were on, and as for any sort of obstruction charges, that's crap. I hired him."

"But Detective Sumner did not," the chief pointed out.

"No, *I* did. Me." I tapped a pointer finger at my chest. "My child was kidnapped, too. Both girls happened to be together … in the custody of Gary's ex-wife." I aimed the little jab at the police chief, too late in realizing it pricked Gary as well.

The ADA's face whipped around to give Gary a hard stare.

"Correct me if I'm wrong, but as a civilian, I had every right to do so. Ziggy has a legal P.I. license to investigate for private citizens." *I hoped.* A quick glance at my sister's nodding head confirmed my assertions.

There was some uncomfortable shifting, and for a moment nobody spoke.

"So, you're alleging that you hired Mr. Zigarelli?" the ADA asked.

"Yes, no alleging."

"How much did you pay him?"

"I don't know—he hasn't invoiced me." I shrugged. "Before he left my house I told him money was no object."

"And to your knowledge, there were no drugs on the boat. And there was no exchange made during your rescue trip?"

Sophie gave an incensed squeak while I gave a short bark of laughter. "Are you freaking kidding me? Of course, no drug deal went down while we rescued my daughter. That is the most asinine thing I've ever heard."

The ADA swiveled to my sister.

Sophie shook her head. "No way. I'm dead set against drugs. And my fiancé will tell you the same thing. Gary can back us up on this."

Gary gave his tie an uncomfortable tug and remained mute. Probably not a good idea to get into the details about the drug addict who was thrown out of their party, left me a few dead rats, and then vandalized my car.

"Gentleman"—the ADA looked at the chief, who'd turned beet red, whether from my direct attack or from closeness in the room I wasn't sure—"from what I've heard, I don't feel there is enough evidence in this case to continue pursuing it. I recommend you move on." With that, she exited the room, allowing a breeze of fresh air to enter the stuffy chamber.

"Hi, Monica."

"Theresa, what are you doing here?" we heard from the hall.

"I'm looking for Sophie Hartland."

Five heads swiveled to my sister. Her eyes widened, and she practically fell out the door. "Here I am, Theresa."

Fifteen minutes later, we sat comfortably around the conference room table as Detective Ramirez typed our statements under the stern supervision of Theresa Candell, our attorney and former client of my sister's. Ziggy spoke in his deep, dulcet tones, providing a succinct accounting of our involvement rescuing the girls. I hoped my sister was paying as close attention as I to Ziggy's simple and relatively brief accounting. He answered the questions with as little embellishment as possible. A tactic I planned to follow.

Ramirez typed the last period and clicked around the screen. "We'll need you to review your statement and sign it. Who's next?" The detective looked between Sophie and me.

"Me," I volunteered.

...

Gary stuck his head in the conference room. The lawyer sat at the head of the table, Ziggy, Sophie and Holly along one side, and

Ramirez by himself on the other. "Excuse me." All heads pivoted and five expressions focused on him; none of them overly friendly. "Can I have a moment, Detective Ramirez?"

"Sure, can I get anyone a cup of coffee?" Ziggy and the lawyer took him up on his offer, the other ladies declined, and the detective brushed past as he exited.

Gary assessed the mood. The lawyer and Ziggy's face remained neutral, but Sophie's frown depicted her unhappiness at this morning's events, and Holly's stiff posture and wary eyes darted around the room suspiciously. He cleared his throat and plowed forward. "Listen, I wanted to apologize for the … misunderstanding this morning with Ziggy. I'm sorry you had to deal with that."

Ziggy gave a brief nod. "No problem."

The demeanors in the room changed slightly with his apology, but distrust, thick enough to spread on toast, remained in the air. Gary shifted his weight. "Also, I realize that in all of the confusion and chaos yesterday, I never took the time to say thank you … for finding the girls. From what I understand, you all played a significant role in returning what is most precious to me. I apologize for the delay in my gratitude."

Ziggy rose and clasped Gary's hand, perhaps a little tighter than necessary. "You take care of that sweet little girl. You hear?"

"Of course."

Sophie, quick to forgive, allowed a smile to peep through as she rose and came around the table to envelope him in a hearty embrace. "We Hartlands take care of our own. I'm just glad the girls are okay."

"Me too," he mumbled.

Throughout the exchange Holly remained seated, although her stance had relaxed and her eyes appeared less wary.

"Holly, can I see you outside for a moment?"

Theresa rose. "What's this about, Detective?"

"Nothing to do with the case. Just about the girls," he assured the lawyer.

"I was about to give my statement," Holly said.

"Don't worry; I'll go next." Sophie winked and tilted her head.

"Don't discuss any aspects of this case with my client. Understood, Detective?" Theresa scowled at him over her half-moon glasses.

"I'll be fine, Theresa. Stay with Soph." Holly pushed back her chair.

He led her into the communal kitchenette and grimaced at the smell of scorched coffee. The room had entries across from one another, and three bistro tables crowded at the far end of the empty room. Gary turned to meet her unsure gaze. She crossed and uncrossed her arms, then played with the pendant on her necklace as she waited for him to speak.

He cut to the chase. "I'm sorry about Ziggy. I wanted you to know I had nothing to do with that."

She crossed her arms again and gave a stiff nod.

Gary rubbed his chin, the mea culpa more difficult to say than he imagined. "Listen, I may have been out of line last night."

Her brows rose. "Ya think?"

He sighed and allowed his arms to relax and hang by his sides. "Okay, you're right, I was way out of line. My only excuse is that stress and lack of sleep clouded my judgment. I wasn't thinking properly. Forgive me."

She blinked and released a breath in a puff. "Okay. I don't like being at odds with you."

Neither did he, and the longer it went on the worse he felt. "Holly, I …" Whatever he was about to say was interrupted by a narcotics detective, dressed in ripped jeans, high-top sneakers, and a black T-shirt, with his badge hanging around his neck.

"Sumner! The man of the hour." He opened the freezer and pulled out a Lean Cuisine box. "Did Kingsley tell you that your

C.I.'s tip panned out?" He popped the frozen entrée into the microwave and punched a few buttons.

"No, I hadn't heard," Gary replied faintly. *Jesus, can't I get five minutes of privacy with this woman?* It seemed every time he turned around, he was tripping over his job.

"Yup." The detective opened the fridge, grabbed a can of Diet Pepsi, and cracked the top with a hiss. "D-back's in custody on an illegal weapons charge while we dig around to pin the Sixth Street murder on him." He took a sip of the soda and finally realized that someone else was in the room and his brows rose.

"Holly, this is Detective McBride in narcotics. Holly's my neighbor," Gary mumbled the introductions begrudgingly.

"Nice to meet you." He stuck out his hand, his dark skin in direct contrast with her light tone as his long fingers wrapped around hers.

"You too. It sounds like you two have some things to discuss, and I'd better return to Ramirez so we can finish up. Detective." Holly nodded at McBride and beat a hasty exit.

"Holly, wait."

She paused and glanced over her shoulder.

"We have unfinished business. Let me take you to lunch afterward."

A smile softened her features, "I'd like that."

Gary watched her delightful bottom in those tight jeans strut down the hall before turning back to find his colleague grinning from ear to ear.

"Sorry, man, didn't realize I was interrupting."

"It's nothing."

The detective snorted and his brows lifted. "Nothing, my ass. You've got it bad. Wish I had unfinished business with her." He licked his lips and winked.

"Piss off, McBride." Gary stomped out of the kitchen with the detective's laughter ringing in his ears.

Chapter Eighteen

Gary sat at the kitchen table as I handed him a plate of steaming pasta. "Careful, it's very hot. I think I left it in the microwave a little too long."

I'd suggested he come over to the house and have some of the leftover pasta I'd put together the afternoon the girls had been kidnapped. Mom baked the pan yesterday, but only two pieces had been eaten.

I sat across from him with my own plate and debated what to say.

"Smells delicious," he said.

"Thanks."

"Your mom going to be okay with the kids today?"

"Sure. Nothing thwarts Dorothy Hartland."

"Is it true she has a talking parrot?"

"Mmm hmm." I blew on a forkful of lasagna.

Our small exchange petered out. A lifetime of events had happened since our steamy snogging session, as Ian would say, and I'd no idea where our relationship stood. Perhaps he wanted our lives to return to what it had been before all of this … hot mess, which made me hesitant to bring up the topic. On the other hand, I didn't want to go back to the status quo. As a matter of fact, just looking at my handsome tablemate made me want to reach across and lick that sauce off the side of his mouth …

Gary shifted in his seat and placed his fork on the plate. "I think we need to talk about what's been happening."

Whoa! I slammed back to earth and my eyes darted to my plate. "Which part, exactly?"

"First, I behaved like an ass. I had no right to criticize you or your actions regarding Claire or the girls. You had no authority to detain Claire, and I'm sorry."

"Thank you for that … and I'm sorry, too. I lied to you, and I shouldn't have done that. Trust is important. People convinced me it was best for the girls. Looking back, now I'm not so sure."

He rubbed the back of his neck. "I realized last night after you left that Claire used to lie to me all the time. It was part of her illness. It made her unreliable, yet through all of this, I still have confidence in you. Possibly because you're the most reliable person in my world and I know that no matter what, you've always got the girls' best interest at heart."

"I do. The girls are everything to me, and I don't just mean Eva. Annie has become just as important to me as my own child. You know that, right? I made a vow to God to show her a mother's love. I mean, I *know* I'm not Annie's mother, but …" Realizing the exact truth of my words, my eyes teared up with emotion. I cleared my throat and dabbed them away with a napkin.

"Shh … I know. Trust me, I know." He reached across the table and his warm hand squeezed mine.

A glass of sparkling water sat at my elbow, and I sipped the bubbly freshness to clear the lump from my throat. It gave me the moment I needed to regain my composure, and I returned the glass to the table with a plunk and a tentative smile.

"Now that we both know how much the girls mean to us, my next question is, what do I mean to you? Where do I fit into Holly Hartland's life?" Gary's gaze surveyed me with both sincerity and wariness.

My mouth bobbed as my brain scrambled the jets to come up with an answer. We'd gone from apologies to confessions, and I wasn't quite sure what he was looking for. Or what I was willing to confess. "Well, I … you're … important. You and Annie …"

That comment was met with raised brows. "I'm talking about us. Not the girls."

"You're important, of course. I mean the other day when we … here in the kitchen, you know." The memory of his lips nipping at my neck spread that delicious tingling sensation down my spine all the way to my toes. My grip tightened around the utensil in my hand. "It was … uh … good." My eyes darted away from his scrutiny down to the plate of lasagna cooling in front of me.

"Just good?"

"Better than. I mean it was," I cleared my throat, "wonderful. Really hot …" I said the last in a whisper. My face burned as I forked a piece of lasagna and proceeded to shove it around my plate. "You were here, you remember."

"I remember." His voice sounded like a gravelly grumble that reverberated deep in his chest. "Honey …"

My gaze rose to meet his dancing eyes.

"I'm going to go out on a limb here and tell you that, as my colleague pointed out, I've got it bad for you."

My breath caught. His directness was so unusual. Not like the cop I knew, the one who tended to play his cards close to his chest.

The merriment turned serious. "And I don't just mean the … physical attraction. It's more than physical. If this kidnapping incident has taught me anything, it's that you mean something to me. More than something." He wiped a hand down his face. "Christ, I'm not good with the words. You mean a lot … a whole lot."

I bit my lip and stared with saucer-like eyes.

"But I have absolutely no idea how you feel. I know my being a cop is an issue, the late nights … the gun … my job interrupting our lives. I felt terrible the other day when I had to leave you after Trey vandalized your car. And cops … well, our track record for relationships isn't the greatest …"

His bald statements revealed an unexpected vulnerability, one I'd never really considered. I'd always thought of Gary as my rock with one-dimensional feelings. Now I realized his feelings ran as deep as anyone's. His training simply allowed him to mask them as effectively as the painted face of a geisha.

"Oh my goodness. Gary, no, stop," I rushed to reassure him. "Your job is important. Do not devalue yourself; you're a damn fine detective. And as for leaving me after the rat incident, it's not as though you left me all alone. My sister was on her way, Officer Mahoney was competently taking care of things, and even Kaitlin stayed until all the reports were complete. Honestly, there wasn't much for you to do. As for the gun … well, yes, you know I have an aversion to them, but I'm working on that. Just give me time."

He opened his mouth, but I plowed on. "The main thing is, I've been comparing you and your job to Omar's, and I've come to realize it's not at all the same. Your personalities differ vastly, and from what I've witnessed in the year since I've known you, you take the 'serve and protect' motto to heart. Being a detective isn't just a job; it's your calling. That's something I could never take away from you. Nobody should. And to be clear, I'm no shrinking violet. I know you saw the panic attack and probably compared me to Claire …"

Gary shook his head and opened his mouth, but once again I didn't allow him to interrupt. I had momentum and needed to keep moving forward. "Wait, I need to get this out. Yes, I've had some issues because of Omar, the anxiety attacks, but having had a tête-à-tête with your ex, I think I can safely say that I pale in comparison. You'll never have to worry about the children when they're with me."

His serious eyes gazed at me, but a glimmer of a smile lifted at the corner of his mouth. "That you do. Trust me, Holly, you are one of the strongest women I know, and I've met some doozies in my line of work. I've never worried about Annie when she's with you, not like I did with Claire."

My face burned at his compliment.

"And thank you for being so accepting about my work. You're correct, being a cop is who I am, and my ex never understood. But what I'm really driving at with this discussion— are you willing to explore a deeper relationship with me? I want to be more than your good friend and neighbor. I want you in my life."

A fist clenched in my stomach, and I stared over the precipice with trepidation but not with fear. I realized my declaration never to get involved with another man after Omar had been crumbling away over the past months. As Gary's warmth, sincerity, and revelations washed over me, the last bits dissipated like smoke up a chimney. "I would have to say … yes. I have feelings for you. Both sexual and emotional."

The gaze that swept across my body went from wary to smoldering in the blink of an eye. He rose from the table and came around. "Perhaps we should explore some of those feelings."

His hand wrapped around my elbow. I rose at the gentle urging and gasped as the tingle in my chest turned south and ignited into a slow burn. "Now?"

"No time like the present. And it's not likely your sister will walk in on us this time."

"Maybe not … but my mom might."

"I'm willing to take that chance if you are. I … oof."

He caught me, stumbling only a step as I hurtled herself at him, throwing my arms around his neck.

"I was so worried my actions would be the end of us," I mumbled into the collar of his sport coat.

He stroked my hair. "No. It's just the beginning."

I gazed at him from beneath my lashes. He framed my face with his hands, gently stroking my cheeks with his thumbs as his lips descended to mine.

* * *

Her lips trembled and he bent his head to capture their softness with his own. They had both tacitly agreed to this, and Gary was determined to take it slow. His touch ran through silky locks and down her neck as gently as handling a china doll. Her lips teased his, and he felt her supple tongue dart out. Taking that as an invitation, he stroked his own tongue through her lips. She moaned as their tongues entwined.

His heartbeat picked up speed. She dropped her head back, allowing him access to the soft recesses of her neck, and he didn't think twice before eagerly exploring the tender flesh. Vaguely, he registered her fingers tugging at the buttons of his shirt, but when her fingers slipped in and swept across his chest, he sucked in a breath as desire bloomed and he hardened.

She was wearing a knit top tucked into her jeans; he tugged it loose and in one swift movement divested her of it. A lacy, black bra with a tiny, white rosette covered her heaving breasts, but before he could inspect further, Holly's frenzied fingers loosened his tie, drawing it overhead and tossing it away before yanking apart the rest of his shirt. A button popped and clinked along the tile floor. Gary divested himself of the rest as she brushed her cheek against the fuzzy, blond curls across his chest.

"You've been working out, haven't you?" she whispered, planting feather-light kisses in a circle around his left nipple.

"At lunch, yes-s," he breathed.

While she busied herself stroking and nibbling, his now-unsteady fingers wrestled with her tiny bra hooks, finally achieving success. Kneading and stroking, he removed the straps until the barrier fell away and allowed him unfettered access to her pebbled, rosy nipples. He rolled one between his thumb and forefinger and she flung her head back, moaning. Replacing his fingers with his greedy mouth, the moans turned to panting.

"Omigod, omigod," she gasped and grabbed his head.

He released the hard nub and moved to lavish his attention on the other one. Her breath quickened to a frantic pace, and he caressed and stroked taking her up higher until she was practically keening his name.

And, before he realized what was happening, the slow foreplay turned into frenzy. She tugged at her belt, unbuttoned her pants, allowed them to drop to the floor, and kicked them aside. Attacking his pants, she tugged ineffectively at the belt for a moment before he pushed her hands away to do it himself. After that, they shed clothes like a dog's coat in the springtime.

Her fingers fondled his hard shaft as his tongue lashed her velvety skin. He walked her back until she bumped into the kitchen island, and then his hands splayed around her torso and he lifted her up on the countertop. She spread her legs and his exploring fingers caressed the silken skin at her thighs and headed north until they found her feminine core. He stroked the swollen, moist folds.

"Please, Gary, now." She moaned and tugged him close, guiding his pulsating shaft into her.

"Holly," he moaned, pushing all the way to the hilt. Crunching his eyes closed, he paused to get his bearings. It'd been a long time since he'd been inside a woman, even longer since he'd been emotionally tied to his sexual partner. The two combined heightened his senses in a way he'd never before experienced. He stroked her again and watched the unrestrained ardor cross her features. She caught her kiss-swollen lip between her teeth. Her rosy nipples stood at attention and her breasts, flushed with desire, urged him to lean down to feast upon the flesh. She gasped and an uncontrollable hunger flooded his system. He took a moment, aware that it would be far too easy to give into his libido and take her like a rutting bull.

"More," her impassioned request whispered through the room.

He began with slow strokes, which she met and, grabbing his backside, increased the tempo.

"More," she begged. The pulse at her neck fluttered in a quick, staccato beat.

Unable to restrain himself any longer, Gary gave into her pleas and the two danced to a rhythm as old as time. They lifted together on the wings of passion until she screamed out his name, tightening around him, and he allowed his own release to fly.

• • •

Our harsh breaths slowed their panting, and the feeling returned to my body as I spiraled back to earth.

My fingers prickled.

The cold countertop pressed into my naked bottom.

Gary's furry chest hair tickled my skin as he draped over me.

My senses gradually registered each of these feelings, but none of them registered as deeply as the sensations that engulfed my heart. I know they say that women have difficulty separating love from sex. Words formed in my mind, but it was this knowledge that made me bite my tongue to keep from blurting out an inappropriate and un-thought-out declaration.

The muffled ringing of Gary's phone broke the silence.

"Shit," he mumbled into my shoulder.

"Do ..." I croaked and swallowed before trying again. "Do you have to get that?"

"Yes. It's my supervisor's ringtone." He righted himself and cupped my cheeks.

"Ah."

"Holly ... I ..."

"Shh." I laid a finger to his lips. "Don't. I understand. Your job means something to this community."

He gave me a hard kiss, then turned to find the phone.

We retrieved our clothes as he spoke to his supervisor, pulling on his pants while securing the phone to his ear with a shoulder. I inferred from the one-sided conversation that our afternoon delight was over. The uneaten lasagna still sat on the table, and I scooped his portion into a plastic container.

The phone call ended, and I held out the container and a fork as he buttoned his shirt. "Take this with you. You'll be hungry later."

"I'm hungry now." He gave me a look that perked up my lady parts again.

"Go," I said with a self-satisfied smile.

"We'll talk tonight."

His lips captured mine one last time before he headed out the door. As it closed, I collapsed on the closest chair. A piece of black caught my eye, and I reached beneath the table and pulled out Gary's tie and my bra wound together. I grinned and unhooked the strap from its mooring. *I wonder when he'll notice it's missing.*

In a way, the phone call interruption gave me time to compose myself and my thoughts. Not only was Gary one of the most important people in my life, but also, if our recent tryst was anything to go by, our sexual compatibility was off the charts. Perhaps I did have a future that would include a man. A man with integrity. A man with golden-brown eyes that could turn steely and make my skin go cold, yet, with the ability of a chameleon, brighten to a warm twenty-year-old bourbon and make my skin burn with desire. A man who would never physically hurt me, but who, I realized, had the ability to emotionally hurt me by withdrawing his … love? Love? Did I say that word? Were Gary's feelings running that deep? He said he wanted our relationship to move forward; he wanted more. *Was he speaking just sexually?* I dismissed that idea. Gary may not love me in the sense that a married couple loves. But he certainly cared for me as a true friend. Perhaps it was a type of feeling that could grow into … I shook my head and returned to my cold lasagna.

Chapter Nineteen

The candles flickered and the chandelier lent a soft glow to the overflowing dining room table. The last bite of pecan pie slid down my throat, and I pushed the plate away, listening with half an ear to the current debate over foreign policy in the Middle East. Sitting back, I groaned and patted my full tummy.

"I don't care how much oil they have, their oppression of women is appalling, and we shouldn't count them as an ally on principle." Sophie thunked her wine glass down for emphasis.

She sat to the right of Ian, who was at the head of the mammoth table. The discussions during the Christmas Eve meal were as varied as the participants. Next to my mom sat her fiancé Harvey, a widower she'd been dating almost as long as Ian and Sophie had been together. Harvey arrived this morning to spend Christmas with us. He was three years retired from a pharmaceutical company and was an avid golfer. To our delight and surprise, Harvey began the dinner by clanking his glass with a spoon and then announcing that he'd asked my mom to marry him. Dorothy had observed my sister and me with a wary smile until whoops of joy flooded the room. A date hadn't been set, but Mom said she'd like to have a simple ceremony at the house and would likely do it before Ian and Sophie's big bash. Ian cracked open the champagne and we toasted the happy couple.

Poppy and Adam were seated across from Gary and me, and next to Poppy sat her mother and stepfather, Hamisi, a beautiful dark-skinned Kenyan. Amalina shared the glad tidings that her latest cancer treatment had come to an end and she'd be able to travel back to Africa with her husband after Poppy and Adam left for their honeymoon in the New Year. More cheers went up, more bottles were opened, and the champagne made another trip around the table.

The girls sat to the right of Gary, and though they may not have understood the importance of the announcements, their excitement over impending Christmas presents made them whoop and clap as much as the rest of us. When Annie asked if she could have some of the bubbly drinks too, Sophie pulled out a bottle of sparkling cider for the girls. Annie pouted that it wasn't the same, and Gary offered to drink it too, but it was really Poppy who came to the rescue by claiming that the champagne tickled her nose and asking for cider.

Gary's parents, Bob and Cora, also known as Pop Pop and Gammy, were assembled at the foot of the table. Bob was a retired cop, and Cora was still working as a professor at a community college in their hometown. The pair had arrived yesterday and planned to stay until New Year's Day. Annie was over the moon with their visit. I'd met them briefly around the time Gary and I had come up with our daycare plan at the beginning of the year. Though he'd visited them, this was the first time they'd been back to LA since that time, and I was looking forward to getting to know them better. Bob was bald on top with white hair circling the circumference of his head, and he had about three inches on Gary. However, as I surveyed the pair, I realized Gary's looks came from his mother. Her freckled skin, prominent nose, and eyes crinkled just like her son's when she smiled. I'd be seeing them again tomorrow when they came over to my house for dinner along with Ian and Sophie.

That was our Christmas Eve table, although now two chairs sat empty since Annie and Eva had abandoned their places immediately after scarfing down their slices of pumpkin pie with extra whipped cream. The pair hunkered down in front of the Christmas tree, and I spied them surreptitiously shaking the wrapped presents. I tapped Gary's arm, which was slung across the back of my chair, and pointed at the pair.

"If you break it, you don't get to keep it," Gary warned with good humor.

Eva dropped the package she'd been holding.

My attention returned to the table to find Adam pouring more of the sparkling cider into Poppy's glass, which I found odd since I knew Poppy enjoyed champagne as much as I did, and with the girls away from the table, there was no longer any need to keep up the charade. I thought about saying something, but instead tilted my head to scrutinize her. Her hair hung against her shoulders in loose curls, and she wore a black dress, which, as usual, set off her svelte frame to perfection. *Nothing seems out the ordinary, yet …*

"Right, Holly?" My sister's voice intruded on my contemplations, but I continued to stare at Poppy's champagne glass.

"What?"

"What do you think?"

"I think … I want to know why Poppy's not drinking tonight."

Adam's arm, which had been leisurely hanging across the back of her chair jerked.

"Seriously?" Sophie's eyes swiveled to our redheaded friend in surprise. "What's up with that?"

Pinkness suffused her features, and for once in her life, Poppy didn't seem to have a quick answer.

"You're … not … are you?" I sat forward in my chair.

"Um …" Poppy licked her lips.

"*Omigod!* How could I have missed it?" Sophie cried and pointed a finger. "You are."

Poppy sighed, then let rip a blinding smile that lit up her face. "Okay, yes. I haven't been to the doctor yet, but I've peed on four different sticks and they all seem to think I'm pregnant."

The table went into an uproar. There were hugs and Adam received his share of male back patting.

"Wait, does this mean you were pregnant at the wedding?" Sophie spoke above the din.

"Apparently so."

"I couldn't be happier for you two." I enveloped Poppy in a hug.

Delight reigned supreme over the gathering. It seemed the upcoming year would be bringing good things. Following Poppy's announcement, the table arrangement realigned itself. Ian disappeared. Adam was booted out of his spot and shooed away, relegating him to the foot of the table with rest of the men while the women converged at the head. The women's high voices sounded like a flock of magpies chattering.

Ian reemerged, carrying a yellow box. "Gentlemen, and ladies who wish to partake, the best from Cuba." He flipped open the lid to reveal a dozen Cuban Cohibas lined up like fat brown pencils.

Gary rubbed his eyes. "I'm not going to ask where you got them, Ian, but today, let's pretend they came from the Dominican Republic."

"Hey, I thought you Yanks were 'normalizing relations.'"

Gary frowned.

"That's what I said. Nothing but the finest from the Dominican Republic." Ian winked and flashed a grin.

"Yuck. You boys take your stink sticks outside, please." Sophie flapped her hand at the men gathered around Ian.

"But, luv, it's cold outside," Ian responded.

"Secondhand smoke is bad for the baby. Light the fire; you'll be fine."

"Back in a moment, mates. Pick your poison while I get the fire lit." Ian trooped outside. Adam, Gary, and Hamisi did that weird cigar routine sniffing and listening to it, while Harvey and Gary's father declined the treat and wandered over to the couch to talk golf.

Amalina launched into the story of Poppy's birth, and I reclined in my chair and recalled last year's Christmas when my sister was still recovering from a bullet wound, put there by my ex-husband who was now marking time in the clink. Eva, only two at the time, and I had moved into Sophie's house, and I had started seeing a shrink to help me get past the abuse I'd endured at Omar's hands. Back then, I'd felt like a grand piano had lifted off my chest and I could breathe. However, I'd also felt like such a failure: jobless, living off my sister who, without a word, paid for our living expenses until I got back on my feet.

Now here I sat, an equal, with a lucrative job I adored. My daughter—scratch that, my daughters—were happy and healthy, and I was surrounded by friends and family I loved and who loved me back. My network of strength and wisdom gathered around this table on this holy night.

To top it off, a man who I considered my best friend was now my lover. It was strange to roll that label around in my head, knowing Gary was so much more to me than that. Without noticing, Gary had become my other half in the past year.

This holiday couldn't be more perfect.

Gary's instincts must have felt my gaze, for he turned and our eyes locked. A jolt of primal electricity shot through me. Gary gave a half smile and wiggled his Cohiba.

A naughty gremlin made me run my tongue along my upper lip, which caused Gary's eyes to bulge like a Bug Out Bob toy. The look was gone in a blink of an eye. I know it was childish, but my feminine ego gave a fist pump, and I smirked as I turned back to the conversation at hand, only to find my sister's level stare looking right at me. My face burned, but instead of looking away, I raised my chin in challenge. She rolled her eyes and cocked her head.

Ian drew her attention as he called for the men to join him, and soon the table was left to the ladies. Eventually, Mom and Mrs. Sumner left us and wandered over to the Christmas tree, involved in their own conversation. The girls climbed into their grandmothers' laps, and from snippets of the conversation that reached my ears, it seemed Mrs. Sumner recounted the nativity story. The golf conversation ceased and the men tuned into the story with rapt attention. Gammy's wrinkled finger pointed to the figurines of the Three Wise Men that hung on the tree, and Eva climbed out of my mother's lap to touch the chubby king riding an elephant.

"Lina if it's a girl," Poppy said, bringing my attention back to the discussion at hand. "What do you think?" She looked expectantly at the group and gripped her mother's hand.

"I love it," Sophie gushed.

"Me too." I grinned.

Amalina nodded and used a napkin to wipe tears from her eyes.

"What if it's a boy?" I asked.

Poppy grimaced. "Adam and I are still working on boy names. We're having a hard time coming to an agreement. I like Blaise or Solomon, but Adam wants to go more traditional, like Richard or James." She sighed.

Eva rubbed her eyes and yawned. I checked my watch and found it was past eight thirty. Knowing it would take a good fifteen to twenty minutes just to bid farewell and pack up the children, I excused myself from the table and, drawing open the back door, I slipped into the frigid night to uproot Gary from his stogie smoking buddies.

As predicted, twenty minutes later, Mom, Harvey, Eva, and I, along with Gary's family, stood in Ian's driveway saying our own good nights since we'd brought two cars and wouldn't see everyone until the following afternoon. Sophie had also come out front with us and was assisting Eva into her car seat. My mother, a natural-born hugger, started the rounds: first Gammy, Gary, and ending with Pop Pop. Since it seemed to be the thing to do, after eyeing each other for a moment, Gary and I entered into a chaste hug, which seemed peculiar because we'd never been huggers before, and now that we'd been intimate, the hug seemed slightly odd. That was, until I relaxed and melted into the embrace.

"Merry Christmas, Holly." His breath tickled my ear and made me shiver.

Before I could respond, he was pushed aside, and I found myself engulfed in Gammy's baby powder-scented embrace. "What a lovely dinner tonight. I'll need to send your sister a thank you note." She disengaged from the hug but kept me close, wrapping her arm around my shoulders. "Now, as for tomorrow, what I can bring—dessert, side dish?" she asked in an undertone, as though sharing a secret.

"Nothing, really. From what I can tell, my mother has filled the refrigerator to capacity, and we will have more than enough food for everyone. You don't need worry about a thing."

"No, no, I must bring something," she fretted. "We've brought a couple bottles of wine from one of our local wineries."

"Perfect." I gave her a reassuring smile.

"Well, if you're sure that's it? No cookies? Deviled eggs?"

"The wine will be fine." I patted the hand at my shoulder.

"If you're sure. Thank you for inviting us."

"It's no problem. I look forward to spending the afternoon with you. And I know the girls would hate to miss sharing their Christmas toys with each other."

"They've become like sisters, haven't they?"

"Well, they do spend a lot of time together."

She pursed her lips, and her green eyes gave me a speculative look before turning them on her son, who was helping Annie get buckled into her booster seat.

"Merry Christmas." I disengaged from the embrace before she could say anything else and beat a hasty retreat to the driver's side of my car.

• • •

Dressed in penguin PJs, Eva hunkered under the covers as Mom read our family's favorite, *'Twas the Night Before Christmas.*

"… to all a good night." Mom snapped the book shut. "Now it's time for little girls to go to sleep." She rubbed noses with Eva and kissed her cheeks, then left the two of us together.

"Mom, will Santa bring me the Frozen Castle I asked for?" Eva asked.

"Well, have you been a good girl?"

She nodded.

"Then, I'm sure Santa will bring it." I tucked the covers around her and the plethora of stuffed animals she'd insisted on bringing to bed, and kissed her soft forehead. "Get to sleep so Santa can come. You know he doesn't come if the children are awake."

She snuggled down. "I love you, Mommy."

"I love you, too." I flipped on her nightlight.

"I can't wait until tomorrow morning," she whispered as I closed the door.

Mom and Harvey were in the living room watching *It's a Wonderful Life*. I popped some popcorn and joined them.

Just past ten thirty, a text message from Gary beeped at me.

You still awake?

Yup. Watching TV with Mom and Harvey.

Can you meet me at the corner?

Sure. What's wrong?

Nothing.

K. See you in a mo.

"Gary needs something. I'll be back in a few."

Mom gave an absentminded wave as her eyes remained glued to Jimmy Stewart running through the streets yelling "Merry Christmas!"

Gary stood in a pool of yellow light on the corner of his street and mine, his hands jammed into his coat pockets.

"What's up?" I stopped in front of him. The lighting shadowed his eyes, but my intuition felt the intense stare. He brushed a lock of hair away from my face and his lips met mine. It was a slow but needy kiss. I was sorry when it ended.

"I've been wanting to do that all night long."

"Uh-huh," was all I could achieve before his mouth descended on mine again. When we finally broke apart, I took a step back, breathing heavily. A neighborhood dog barked, and it occurred to me that we were standing on a public street—granted not a busy one, but in our neighborhood and public nonetheless. "I kind of feel like a teenager, sneaking out to neck with my boyfriend."

Teeth flashed at me and he drew a gentle finger down my nose. "When I caught you watching me, I thought, 'This is a perfect night.'"

My breath caught. "We must have been communicating telepathically, because I was thinking the same. So much has changed for the better since I arrived looking like a mangy mongrel at my sister's doorstep. Remember?"

Gary's chest expanded. "I remember."

"Things finally seem to be falling into place." I sighed, hugged him close, and laid my head in the crook of his collarbone.

"Holly … do you think you might, one day, make other more drastic changes?"

I looked up. "What do you mean?"

His jaw flexed, and I could tell he measured his words carefully before speaking. "Would you … consider marrying again?"

My breath caught and the hand rubbing my back froze.

I didn't allow my brain a moment to think but instead permitted my heart to speak. "Yes," I whispered.

"Good." The rubbing recommenced.

"What about you?"

"Of course."

"When?" I cocked my head.

"When, what?"

"When do you think you might be ready to remarry?"

Gary screwed up his mouth and seemed to contemplate the question. "June."

"June, huh?" I laughed. "That's rather specific."

"June's a nice time to get married."

"Yes, you're right. June is a beautiful month to marry."

Our eyes locked. The smile slid off my face. Our subconscious seemed to be asking what the other meant but hesitated to speak aloud.

"What … are we saying?" He broke the silence.

"It depends; what are you asking?" I chewed my bottom lip.

His chest expanded as he sucked in a breath. "Holly Hartland, I love you and think that we make a great family … together."

"Okaaay. I love you too." My heart flooded with joy at his declaration of love, but I was still unclear where we were going with this discussion.

"So, do you think you can marry me … in June?"

Finally, there it is. My heart and my stomach did a flip-flop dance, and it took all my effort not to break out into a jaw-cracking smile. "I'm not sure …"

Gary stiffened and went to take a step back, but I held him close. "I'll have to see if my wedding planner is available."

He grunted and, scooping me into his embrace, spun me around beneath the glowing yellow light as joyful merriment and happiness flooded out of me in gleeful giggles.

My head spun dizzily when my feet finally returned to the pavement, and I held tightly as I regained my equilibrium.

"That was a most unconventional proposal." I smiled.

Gary released me and, stepping back, dropped to one knee, and then grasped my left hand in his.

"No, no, no. Get up, get up." I cut him off before he could speak. "It's far too cold out for down-on-one-knee proposals. Besides, our lives … no, our relationship has been unconventional thus far; let's not ruin the moment by becoming conventional now." Laughingly, I tugged at his hand.

His eyebrows knit. "Are you sure?"

"Of course." I tugged harder.

"I love you." Our voices melded as once again his strong embrace wrapped around me.

"Our families are going to think we're nuts, considering we haven't even been boyfriend-girlfriend and we're going straight to engagement," I pointed out.

"First, I have a feeling your sister saw this coming. Second, my mother, quite officiously asked me tonight when I planned to make an honest woman out of you."

"You told her we were sleeping together?"

"Hell, no. She seemed to divine it. Perhaps she caught the sexy lip-licking incident and my reaction to it."

My face burned with mortification. "Will they be upset?"

He nuzzled my hair. "Mmm, you smell good.."

"*Gary.*"

"I doubt it. What about yours?"

Gary was right about Sophie—she wouldn't be surprised. "Mom seems to adore you and Annie. So, though she'll likely tell me not to rush, I think she will be pleased."

"I know that Annie will be over the moon, but what about Eva?"

"Eva"—I sighed—"was recently telling me that Annie is her sister. When I explained that she was a good friend and would only be her sister if you and I got married, she asked when that would happen."

"What did you say?"

"I told her I didn't know and we'd talk about it later."

"Now you can tell her: in June."

"June … omigod." I put a hand to my mouth. "With Mom and Harvey announcing their engagement, I've just realized that we'll have three Hartland weddings next year."

"And three very lucky men." He grinned.

I got all squishy inside and we didn't speak for a while. Even though the wintry temperatures had dropped and the winds kicked up, our body heat kept the chill at bay. Bright lights swept past us, and the beep-beep of a friendly horn finally broke us apart.

"I guess I'd better get back home," I said with reluctance.

"Yeah."

Neither of us moved.

"Seriously, our families will be wondering what happened."

He nodded.

"Merry Christmas, Gary." I rose on my toes and gave him a quick kiss.

"Merry Christmas, my love."

Epilogue

Gary slid the rose gold band that matched the antique diamond engagement ring he'd given me on Christmas Day on my finger as he intoned the time-honored pledge. The set had belonged to his great-grandmother, and, since Claire had insisted on a modern setting, he'd been sitting on it, with plans to pass it along to Annie when the time came. Now Annie or her children would get it in due course. Cora told us the set carried luck, because her grandmother was married for sixty-two years before her husband passed away, and she continued to wear the rings until the day she died at the age of ninety-one.

Eva and Annie, our little flower girls, crowded around Gary and me, much too interested in the ceremony, refusing to stand passively at my sister's side. I didn't care. My cheeks physically hurt from smiling so much, but try as I might, I couldn't stop the action. When I woke this morning, for some reason, *The Sound of Music* kept running through my head. My heart was so full of joy and happiness it took both mental and physical strength to keep from inappropriately bursting out into song. Mom's soft sniffling from behind brought me back to the matter at hand, and I slipped the plain silver band onto my new husband's hand.

The wedding turned out to be relatively small with only sixty guests—a far cry from my sister's two months earlier at 410 but more than Mom and Harvey's guest list back in May, which came in at a conservative seventeen and consisted of his family and ours.

Before I knew it, the recessional organ music resounded through the church, and we floated back down the aisle—flashes popping—as husband and wife. A grinning Poppy stood, with one hand resting on the basketball-sized baby bump, at the end of the walkway, her iPhone trained on us. Today she played both guest and planner; however, I made it quite clear that once the luncheon reception got underway, her planning duties were to come to an end, and I expected her to relax and get off her feet. She looked stunning in pregnancy, and though she still had another two months to go, I had no doubt a protective Adam would see to Poppy's heeding my requests.

Upon exiting the chapel doors, my new husband, his eyes dancing, pulled me to him. "Hello, wife."

"Hello, husband." I snuggled into his loving embrace, a mantle I determined never shed.

"Eva, this means we're real sisters now," Annie said with excited tones.

"Is it true, Mommy?" Eva tugged on my dress.

"Yes, pumpkin. You and Annie are sisters now." I smiled down at her adorable face.

"Yay." She promptly threw her basket of flower petals in the air and proceeded to run in circles chanting, "I have a sister, I have a sister."

Annie dropped her pillow that had carried our rings and joined her new sister's dance.

"Slow down, girls," I called.

Unfortunately, Murphy's Law played its role. The girls, not paying attention to one another, slammed together, bonking their heads with an audible crack, and then proceeded to fall in their pretty dresses onto the grass. Little girl wails promptly carried their way up to the heights of the church spire.

Gary and I shared that telepathic look that only parents understand. "I'll take care of this," he said releasing me.

"No." I laid a hand on his forearm. "We'll take care of this."

More from This Author
(From *Planning for Love* by Ellen Butler)

The incessant ring of the phone interrupted my brief commune with the now-lukewarm latte. My hand jerked, and the creamy mixture sloshed over the side, spilling onto my black pants. I knew today would be busy, but it wasn't yet nine and this was the fifth time the phone had interrupted me.

Damn. I pulled a tissue out of the box on my desk and wiped at the stain, hoping it wouldn't be visible when it dried, because I didn't have time for a trip back to the house to change. The phone continued its insistent ring as I shuffled a pile of papers aside in search of my headset. Obviously, this morning wasn't going as I'd originally planned. I located the little black earpiece buried under a pile of menus, hooked it on, and pressed the answer button on my desk phone.

"Go for Poppy," I answered while at the same time pulling up an email from tonight's restaurant manager.

"It's Cody."

"Where are you? Are you coming in to the office today, or going directly to the venue?" I typed a quick response to the restaurant manager's question while Cody spoke.

"I'm on my way into the office right now. I got an email this morning from the M.O.B. of the Moscowitz wedding, and they don't want the white, horse-drawn carriage. They're asking if it can be painted apricot to match the orchids in the bride's bouquet. She's even gone to the paint store and picked up swatches. I didn't want to respond until I got your thoughts on it."

"That woman is off her rocker. They can't afford that; they're going to have to mortgage their house by the time this wedding is done. I'm sorry you have to deal with her."

"No problem. It's nothing I can't handle, and she won't be the last. But what do you think I should do? Head this scheme off at the pass, or …?"

I sighed. "No. You have to at least ask the question. Call Sandra at Classic Carriages and see if they'll accommodate the request. Have her give you an estimate on the cost to paint the apricot and repaint the carriage back to white. Inflate it by twenty percent because it always costs more than anticipated, and then tell the M.O.B what the price would be for her latest notion. Make sure to cc the F.O.B. I have a feeling once Mr. Moscowitz sees the bottom line, he'll put an end to it, but if they're willing to pay, we'll make it happen."

The other line rang.

"I've got another call. Let's touch base at ten to make sure everything is set for the parties tonight."

"Ten it is."

I hung up on Cody, my second in command, and pressed the blinking light to my other line.

"Go for Poppy."

"Go for Poppy? What the hell is *that*? I think this town is getting to you. You sound like a snooty, high-powered agent or something." My best friend, Sophie Hartland, laughed at me through the phone lines.

I brought up another email, an invoice. "Hey, Soph. My phone's been ringing off the hook this morning. Cody and I both have Valentine's parties tonight, and everyone seems to be having meltdowns over inconsequential details. What's up?"

"I said yes,"

I forwarded the email to Rachel, my bookkeeper, approving the invoice and directing her to pay it. "Yes to what, doll? Did you score a new hotshot client?" I asked in a distracted voice.

"I said yes, to Ian."

My fingers froze over the keyboard, and I sucked in a breath. "Are you saying what I think you're saying?"

"Yes!" She let out a very un-Sophie-like squeal.

"Omigod, omigod!" I jumped out of my chair and let out a un-Poppy-like squeal. The headset ripped off my head and fell to the floor. I snatched the handset from the cradle. "You're going to be Mrs. Ian O'Connor."

"I know. Can you believe it?"

"It's about time. You've been torturing that poor man since Thanksgiving. I still don't understand what took you so long to say yes."

"C'mon, Poppy, I told you I didn't want to jump into another marriage and have it end up like the first. If Ian and I are getting married, I'm going in eyes open. I'm not a young, twenty-something any more. I'm thirty. I need to make decisions like a thirty-year-old."

Sophie was an interior designer. We met more than six years ago at a party I was running; she moved a few things around on a tablescape, added some of the hostess's collection of crystal balls, and an "eh" table setting turned into a "wowee." I hired her on the spot to design private, themed parties. But with her own design company taking off, she had less and less time to give to my party planning business.

"Sure, sure. So have you picked a date yet?"

Sophie's laughter floated through the lines. "We haven't gotten that far. I just got off the phone with Ian a few minutes ago. I'm driving over to a client's house as we speak. You're the first on my speed dial."

"Wait a minute, you said yes to Ian over the phone?"

"I told you he's been asking me at all sorts of odd times. So, if he's going to pop the question over the phone, that's how he'll get his answer. I promised to swing by the set during lunch."

"I hope you're planning something nice for dinner tonight."

"You bet I am. It'll be served in a red teddy with whipped cream and a cherry on top."

I hooted. "Ooh, la, la. Naughty, naughty."

"What about you and Rich? Any plans? Or are you working?"

"I'm running a Valentine's gig in Beverly Hills, but we're planning a late-night rendezvous. As a matter of fact, I'm heading over to his place around lunchtime to drop off some champagne and caviar."

"Nice."

"So, does he have a ring?" I asked.

"Knowing Ian's persistence for the past few months, I would say it's not out of the realm of possibility." Sophie let out another breezy laugh "I don't really know."

"Well, I'm going to have my hands full planning such a high-profile wedding."

"About that …"

"Don't tell me you're planning your own wedding, Sophia Hartland. That bird won't fly."

"No, I'm not planning it. But, neither are you."

It felt like a punch to the gut. I couldn't believe my best friend didn't want me to plan her wedding. I plopped down in my chair. "What?"

"Cody's planning it, because you're going to be in it. You're going to be my maid of honor."

My breath whooshed out. "Aw, Sophie. That's … that's …. I don't know what to say." My throat clenched, and I coughed to clear away the sentimentality.

"Say, yes, you goof."

"But what about your sister?"

"She got to be my maid of honor the first time around. She'll be a bridesmaid this time. She's a single mom now, and she won't have time to do all the maid of honor stuff. Besides, you earned the position. After all, it was you who introduced me to Ian,"

Ian played Ryder McKay on the cop show *L.A. Heat.* At one of my swanky birthday parties for a Hollywood director, Ian commented on the retro theme Sophie had designed, and I offered to introduce him. Not long after that, Ian hired Sophie to redesign his own home, top to bottom. He doggedly pursued her, and eventually she gave in to the steamy chemistry they shared. At Thanksgiving he popped the question, but she turned him down and instead offered a compromise. She moved into his place, and as Soph would say, "they'd been living in sin" ever since.

"So, are you in?" she asked.

"Of course."

"Good, that's settled. You can plan the engagement party."

"Just tell me when and where."

"I'll get back to you."

My cell phone rang.

"And that's my cue," Sophie said. "We'll talk later. You have a lip-smacking good night with Richard."

"Thanks. You, too, and congrats, girlfriend. That's the best news I've heard all day. You and Ian will make beautiful children."

"Hey, hey, one thing at a time." She hung up, laughing.

• • •

My pearl-gray Lexus SUV rolled to a stop in front of Rich's ultra-modern two-story home. I keyed into the house, entering the chrome and white, vaulted foyer and met silence.

Hmm, Rich must have forgotten to set the burglar alarm this morning.

The red flats I wore quietly slapped against the black marble floors in the kitchen where I placed a Trader Joe bag on the quartz countertop. I opened the fridge and unloaded the sack. A bottle of champagne slid onto the bottom shelf, caviar and Brie above it, and lastly, strawberries and whipped cream on the top shelf. The

stainless steel fridge closed with a whisper-soft click. As I folded
the paper bag, my eyes lit on Richard's keys lying on the breakfast
bar. I put the bag aside and picked up the keys. They dangled
between my thumb and forefinger, and I stared at the Infiniti
emblem on the ring.

He's here.

My eyes traveled to the ceiling. The keys dropped back onto the
counter with a clink. Something—call it woman's intuition—kept
me from hollering out his name. Instead, I noiselessly climbed
the stairs and proceeded to the back of the house where Rich's
mammoth master bedroom lay.

The door was shut, and as I approached, a feminine giggle met
my ears. "Ooh, lookee here. That's a big weapon you're packin',
cowboy."

"Well climb on up there, girl, 'cause it's cocked and ready to
fire." Rich's smooth voice responded.

A breath hissed between my teeth. Muffled moans and titters
intermingled with the bed's creaking. My hand rested on the
doorknob, and I debated whether I should enter. Deciding I didn't
need to torture myself by seeing what was going on behind that
door, I turned on my heel and stalked down the hall. I sailed past
the guest room, paused, and backed up to stare at the brand-new
comforter and goose down pillows I'd purchased from Sophie last
week to freshen up the space for an upcoming visit from Rich's
brother. Fury flashed, and my feet moved of their own volition to
the bed, where I yanked off the comforter and pillows. Gathering
the fluffy mass into my arms, I tossed it over my shoulder, and
stalked down the stairs.

Step, step. *How did this happen to me?* Step. Step. *No good,
cheating sonofabitch!* Step, step, step. *If he thinks he'll get away with
this, he's got another think coming.*

Unfortunately, midway through the internal tirade, the little
Jiminy Cricket sitting on my shoulder reminded me this wasn't

the first time I'd been cheated on, and I paused at the last two steps. I had a habit of collecting "bad boys" with commitment issues. The last fool who'd cheated on me found himself locked out of our hotel room in Hawaii, all his crap in a plastic dry cleaning bag sitting by the door at four in the morning. I shook my head to erase the memory. Right now wasn't the time to think about the past. Not when confronted with the present treachery.

I threw the mess of bedding by the front door and stared down at it. Contrary to what people might think, my anger didn't match my fiery red hair. Instead of flashing, screaming rage, I tended to bank my ire into cold, tundra-like fury. Moreover, when it came to cheating bastards, I refused to turn into a lump of crying mess … well, not until after extracting a bit of payback. My brain ticked away, forming and subsequently discarding revenge schemes until I realized one was staring me in the face; something I remembered from a movie. I scooped up the goose down pillows and tiptoed to the kitchen, although considering the howls and yehaws I'd heard coming from the bedroom, there was little need for stealth.

Fifteen minutes later, the comforter, champagne, and other assorted odds and ends I'd brought to the house were keeping company in the front seat of my car. The trap was set. Plastic wrap attached with Scotch Tape to two steel pillars zigzagged across the kitchen entryway. It dripped with honey and two kinds of syrup, the cheap, sticky kind from the grocery store that came in a plastic bottle shaped like a cabin. Richard, the bastard, loved that stuff. I'd slashed open the two pillows and denuded them of their feathers. Their white fluffiness created a small mountain on a side table I'd pulled up just for the occasion. A big box fan that Rich normally kept in the garage sat behind the pile of feathers.

I lit a rolled piece of paper, climbed atop the counter, and waved it below the fire alarm. It took about thirty seconds before the screeching pierced the relative quiet. I dropped the burning paper into the stainless steel sink—after all, I didn't want to burn the man's house down—and placed myself next to the fan.

I wonder if he'll put on a pair of pants. It didn't take long to answer my question.

My slimy, cheating *ex*-boyfriend, buck naked and still sporting a woody at half-mast, stumbled into the coated plastic wrap, which detached from its tenuous Scotch-Taped hold and wrapped around him. He pulled the plastic off and his eyes lit on me in shock and confusion.

"Poppy?" He called over the shrill alarm. "What the hell?"

I squinted and allowed a wicked smile to cross my features. With a gentle flick, the fan turned to high. It succeeded much better than expected. A big clump of feathers moved, en masse, to land on his sticky torso and nether regions. The rest of the feathers blew in a willy-nilly whirlwind and attached to his face, shoulders, and legs.

"Damn it!" he shouted, spitting feathers out of his mouth.

I couldn't help myself; I held up my cell and snapped a photo. The ringing of the house phone added to the cacophony of noise.

I shot past him and tore up the stairs, knowing I had a very short window of opportunity to get my things and make a clean getaway. A naked bimbo with enormous, cartoon-like breasts screeched and pulled the sheet up to her neck. She couldn't have been more than twenty-one, if that. I ignored her and went directly to the bathroom, searching for my favorite silver drop earrings. Luckily, they sat on the shelf where I'd left them two days ago. A few pieces of my clothing rested, neatly folded, in a drawer in the big walk-in closet. I dumped the trash out of the wastebasket, stuffed everything into it, and zipped out, ignoring the screeching blonde on my way.

Back at the kitchen, Rich plucked at feathers surrounding his nose and mouth while yelling at the security company over the noise into the phone. He sneezed, and a giggle bubbled up my throat. I had already retrieved my own house key from his key ring, but I took a moment to remove his from mine and chuck it onto the marble floor by his feet. We both watched as it slid past him underneath the refrigerator. Using my middle finger, I blew him a kiss, flipped my red curls over my shoulder, flung open the front door, and strutted triumphantly to the car.

The smile of satisfaction remained glued to my face well into the evening as I went about my duties, making sure the Valentine's Day party flowed successfully into the night. I ignored the repeated calls from Rich and laughed every time his feathered photo popped up on my phone when he called.

It wasn't until driving home at 2:00 a.m. in my silent car that the pain of betrayal caught up. Visions of happy Valentine's couples dancing and kissing ran through my head, and my sweet revenge on scum-sucking Richard left a hollowness in my gut. Earlier in the day, I had desperately wanted to call Sophie to crow about the successful retribution; now I wanted to cry on her shoulder as it hit me that my status, once again, had returned to singlehood. I held off contacting her, because I didn't want to rain on her engagement parade with the sordid tale of Rich's cheating.

Unchecked tears slid down my cheeks as I keyed into the house. My head whirled with painful "what if" emotions, and I knew I had to talk to someone. Sophie was out, and it would be too late to call Cody or anyone else for that matter, so I fired up my laptop.

To: Adam from Hawaii
From: Poppy Reagan
Subject: Cheating Bastards

Adam,

    I know it's been awhile since we've communicated. I'm sorry. It's been a bad day. Remember that guy I'd been dating, hereinafter to be referred to as Detestable Richard? I found Detestable Richard in bed today with a young blonde with huge boobs. Don't worry, I took my revenge; see attached photo.

Perhaps you're not the right person to be telling this to, but I'm at a low point. It's the middle of the night, all my girlfriends are asleep or having wild gorilla sex, and it's just hit me that the man I've been sleeping with cheated on me on Valentine's Day. Valentine's Day, for crying out loud! Who *does* that? What is wrong with men? How do I attract bastards like Detestable Richard? You're a man—are all men pre-programmed to cheat? Or is it just to cheat on me?

A plastic surgeon passed me his card tonight. Maybe I should go in for a consult to enhance my bust. Perhaps cantaloupes for breasts keep the cheaters away. You're a man, you've seen the goods, tell me the truth. I know I'm skinny. Do I need to get a boob job?

Okay, enough blathering and feeling sorry for myself. How's it going with the schoolteacher? Still all flowers and candy? Did you do something romantic for V-day? The way to a woman's heart is to listen and always compliment her, and don't friggin' cheat! Don't forget, Adam. Don't be a cheater! It's bad! Very, very bad! Now I'm going to drown my sorrows in a bottle of Scotch.

Thanks for listening to me whine.

Your loser friend,

Poppy

• • •

Adam had five minutes before his first patient, which gave him just enough time to check his private email account and maybe clear out some of the spam. He logged in and scanned the subject lines. Delete. Delete. Delete. His mouse paused at an email from a woman. No, not just any woman, a magnificent woman with a smile that could light up Broadway, pearlescent skin that glowed in the moonlight, and the most glorious red hair he'd ever wrapped his hands around.

He'd happily played her rebound guy, and his vacation in Hawaii had turned into an unforgettable, passionate, fun-loving week. Afterward, he reluctantly returned to his life in Ohio. However, to his pleasure, Poppy started a fiery electronic flirtation. The attraction he'd felt during their trip in Hawaii was still in full gear, and he encouraged her to come out for a visit. But to his regret, only a few weeks after their tryst, Poppy began dating a new guy, a schmucky casting something-or-other. As her relationship with this guy grew more serious, Adam backed off and eventually turned his sights elsewhere. Their sexy flirtation tapered off and turned friendly.

With mixed emotions, he opened the email and skimmed its contents. He immediately saw through the sarcasm and humor and could tell she was hurting more than she admitted. His gut clenched at this asshole's perfidy. Honestly, he had no idea what a good thing he had going with Poppy. From her initial emails, Adam had feared that Detestable Richard was a shady character. Maybe it was his prejudice against the Hollywood scene, or perhaps it was the fact her best friend warned her about this guy and she'd ignored it. Ultimately, Rich's cheating didn't come as a shock to Adam.

Oh, good Lord! Implants? What was she thinking? Implants would seriously mar her stunning, athletic figure. Her breasts, though small, fit her body to perfection, and they were so incredibly sensitive, he remembered with a smile. Implants could ruin those lovely, rosy nipples. *I have to tell her to put a stop to that crackbrained idea.*

His curiosity piqued, Adam clicked on the picture icon attached to the email. Patients in the neighboring exam rooms probably heard his uproarious laugh, and he tried to tone it down a notch. The photo showed a guy who looked like a half-plucked chicken-man, and he was *pissed. Damn, that woman is creative. I hope to never get on her bad side.*

The phone at his elbow rang. "Good morning, Georgia."

"Morning to you, too, Dr. Patterson. Something funny?"

"Just a joke a friend sent to me."

"Your first appointment has arrived."

"Thank you. Have the nurse take him back and check the vitals. I'll be with him in a minute."

Adam typed a quick email back to Poppy. He hoped it would cheer her up. As he signed out of his Yahoo account, his mind began turning over ideas. Could he get Poppy back into his life on a more permanent basis and not be seen as the "rebound guy" this time around?

Adam pushed back against his chair and stretched his arms over head. It had been almost a month since he and Sarah had broken up. Sarah had given him an ultimatum to get engaged because her biological clock was ticking. He wanted to continue dating a few more months to expand their relationship and revisit the conversation at a later date. They fought, and Sarah refused to wait. A week after she dumped him, Adam heard she was dating a tax accountant.

Ouch, that hurt.

Now things might be looking up.

As Adam walked down the hall to his first patient, his mind worked on a plan to get his California honey on a plane out to Ohio to reignite their fiery flirtation.

Praise for *Planning for Love*:

"I was in stitches reading what happened ... this author has the golden pen when it comes to comedy writing. I laughed, cried, and cheered as Adam and Poppy came together."—4 stars, Cocktails and Books

"What a fun and entertaining read, with the perfect amount of romance and heat."—5 Stars A Beautiful Book Blog

"Ms. Butler is a master at sexual tension in this delightfully comedic story that portrays the pitfalls of dating perfect strangers."—4 stars, *InD'Tale Magazine*

Also by Ellen Butler:

Heart of Design

Praise for *Heart of Design*:

"Loved all the characters in the book: Ian and his Irish accent, Poppy, her mom and the squawking bird ringtone, and the sister Holly. The secondary story line with Holly added intrigue to the book. All in all a must read!"—5 stars, Harps Romance Book Review

"I know what you are thinking. 'Bah, same old, same old.' But it wasn't, trust me on this ... Have you ever read one of those books where you go, 'What the hell was she/he thinking?" Yeah, this isn't one of them. The characters make smart choices, because the drama is generated from actual events, not manufactured from emotional outbursts. Plus, the dialogue and characters were spot on. I will read more of this author in the future."—4 stars, Musings and Ramblings

"Ellen Butler has written a witty, fast-paced romance that was just a pure pleasure to read. I could easily hear Ian's deep Irish brogue as his flirting made Sophie blush all over. It's the mark of a great writer and I look forward to reading more stories like this one." —4 stars, Reader's Favorite

In the mood for more Crimson Romance?
Check out *Southern Comfort by Amie Louellen* at
CrimsonRomance.com.